The
Traitors

BOOKS BY DEBORAH HILL

The Kingsland Series
This is the House
The House of Kingsley Merrick
The Heir

The Prelude Series
The Pretender
The Hostage

EDITED BY DEBORAH HILL

Recollections of a Cape Cod Mariner:
Elijah Cobb, 1768–1848

The
Traitors

DEBORAH HILL

NORTH ROAD
PUBLISHING

For Stephen

Contents

Author's Note

This small book is the third in a series of novels that include, in counterpoint, the tensions that led to the American Revolution. Creating this series was not my original intention. In fact, *The Prelude* Series created itself.

The first book published, *The Pretender*, was set in Boston in the year 1765, when the English Parliament levied the Stamp Tax on its American colonies. Quickly resistance arose, led by Samuel Adams. This is something nearly everyone who is interested in American history knows. But Adams is not the focus of this novel. Rather, it concerns a young woman who schemes to enter Boston's upper-class society by presenting herself as an English aristocrat. We only have glimpses of Adams working in the background, reminding his fellow citizens that they were being taxed without representation. We never meet him.

Once *The Pretender* was finished, our family took a vacation to Nova Scotia. I had not realized how much of its history was connected to early America including the Acadian Expulsion, brought on by the approaching war with France. And then I found an amazing story in the deepest recesses of the Dartmouth College Library, about the rescue of a group of Acadian prisoners by their Indian allies. *The Hostage* was inspired by these things. And while it is not about Samuel Adams, it does include, as a matter of background information, certain clashes with Parliamentary authority that left a permanent distrust in the minds of certain colonists—including him.

I went no further until I retired and began working on it again with the help of the internet. Then I began to realize that since *The Hostage* alluded to the early political career of Samuel Adams, between the two novels, *The Hostage and The Pretender*, much of his life story had emerged without my even realizing it.

I was compelled to continue.

Easier said than done! A third novel would have to be about the build-up to the Tea Party and the role of Sam Adams in it. But what sort of protagonist could I invent through whose eyes we would learn of his schemes and plots? I'd have to develop a new background for such a character, a new set of circumstances that would locate him or her in that time period, between the repeal of the Townshend Acts in 1770 and the initiation of the Tea Act in 1773. As it turns out, most of the time nothing at all was happening. Everybody was satisfied with the status quo. Everyone except Adams, who saw that the remaining small tax on tea was a Trojan horse.

I was stalled. Until a friend mentioned that "alternative history" is an active enterprise these days. He explained that you can't change known facts, but you can invent new ones if they don't interfere with reality as we know it.

The proverbial light instantly shone at the end of the proverbial tunnel. In a few weeks, a draft emerged—short, sweet, and to the point.

Now, many drafts later, I present *The Traitors*, without a new protagonist but with many of the old ones taking a role to move the reader forward from the Stamp tax, through the Townshend Acts, and straight into the debacle known as The Tea Party.

And, with the help of "alternative history," *The Prelude* series is now complete.

Deborah Hill

1766

CHAPTER ONE

The Proposal

Stanwickshire, England.

The country castle of Sir Edmond Bellingham, Earl of Stanwick, was a gray behemoth. It rose up from the English countryside in unabashed demonstration of its inhabitant's importance. But Ebin Worthington thought it cold. Compared to the smaller wooden mansions of home, it had no appeal. His own sat elegantly on its lot in Boston, painted yellow with green shutters and flowers by the front door, warm at the outset. Why would anyone want to live in a stone mausoleum like this, if such comfort and welcome could be had?

An unsmiling man in livery admitted him to the castle and took his card away. He waited in the spacious ante-chamber, hung with coats of arms and portraits of ancestors. A suit of armor stood propped up under the rising stairs.

The unsmiling man reappeared. "Follow me, if you please."

He followed and was shown into a small receiving room where a spirited fire threw warmth both material and aesthetic. Sir Edmond rose with Ebin's card in one hand, his other outthrust in welcome. "How do you do?"

"My Lord." Ebin took the proffered hand while bowing. "You come well recommended, er, Mr. Worthingham." "Worthington," Ebin corrected. "Ah, yes. Mr. er, Worthington." Most likely the Earl was not often confronted by anyone who was not at least a 'Sir'. Commoners did not often, if ever share his fire. But Ebinezer's letter of introduction, sent on ahead of his visit today, was unique.

"Would you enjoy a glass of brandy?" Bellingham asked.

"Perhaps it would be as well if you heard why I am here, My Lord, and then decide if you'd like to drink with me." Ebin smiled a little as he offered this outstanding example of New World churlishness.

The Earl did not smile in return. "Well, then, at least have a seat." He gestured toward a leather-covered couch placed before the fire. The two men sat as far apart as was possible. "Proceed, Mr. Worthington."

"Lord Bellingham, are you acquainted with displeasure in the colonies over Parliament's recent attempt to tax them?"

"Of course."

"There is concern, among some of us, about the manner in which resistance to it has been organized."

"Have to expect resistance, Mr. Worthington. No one likes taxes, But the recent war with France has increased the indebtedness of the Crown three-fold. What would you have us do?"

Bellingham's eyebrows rose in question.

"Did you know, sir, that immediately upon hearing about the tax, displeased representatives of all the colonies met in a congress and wrote a petition to the King to have the Stamp Act rescinded?"

"Really!" the Earl drawled. "Just a bit presumptuous, I'd say." He considered the matter further. "I doubt such a petition was ever shown His Majesty. No need for distress."

"The point is, sir, that a congress was assembled. A petition was written and sent by a unified group representing all the colonies. Something like that has never happened before."

"Well, I can see how that might seem threatening to those of you loyal to the king," Bellingham nodded. "But . . ."

"There's more. These resisters plan a boycott of British goods. They are convinced that if your merchants are threatened with bankruptcy, they will persuade Parliament to rescind the Stamp Act."

"And you actually believe this boycott will happen?"

Ebin worked a finger up under his wig, scratched. "I believe it is already in effect. But, sir, if the Loyalists make it a point to buy British, a boycott would be neutralized."

"There are many of them, then?"

"Indeed, there are. And my associates and I believe they must be convinced that buying British is critically important—both now and in the future."

"You believe opposition to the Stamp Tax will continue?"

"I believe it will grow, sir. Leading it is a Boston politician who seems determined to undermine royal authority."

"Oh?" Bellingham's eyebrows rose again. "And this politician has a following?"

"Indeed he does."

"Who is he?"

"A fellow called Samuel Adams."

"Perhaps this Adams person should be offered a baronetcy," Bellingham mused. "And money, in exchange for shutting up. Wouldn't that work?"

"Seems unlikely, My Lord. He is poor, but his followers contribute to his cause and his wife collects the contributions and uses them carefully. I think he would not be interested in either a title or money. Besides, he thinks all men are created equal."

"Whatever gave him that idea?" Bellingham scoffed. "And the Loyalists. Adams does not persuade them?"

"They are busy about their lives and do not necessarily read *The Gazette*, which prints what Adams writes."

"Surely there are Royalist newspapers."

"The mob makes cowards of them. But if their offices were elsewhere than Boston, my associates and I believe they would be more forthcoming in their support of Parliament."

Bellingham said nothing, only watched.

Ebin surged on. "You see, My Lord, we are convinced that the colonies must have leaders around whom Loyalists can gather, to counter-balance those men who actively oppose Parliament's decisions. Leaders to show them that buying British is important and will continue to be important in the future. Leaders who will keep them informed of the facts, on both sides of the water."

"What about the governors? Cannot the Loyalists rally around them?"

Ebin responded with a derisive snort. "I'm sure I needn't point out that all the royal governors are aristocrats, appointed by His Majesty. They are more concerned about pleasing him than those whom they govern."

Bellingham looked doubtful, but pried himself off the low-slung couch, stomped over to the sideboard where decanters of various spirits were lined up. "Now that I've heard the reasons for your being here, Mr. Worthington, I think it's time for a little libation. Will you have brandy or scotch?"

Ah! Success! "Have you any rum?" Ebin asked hopefully.

"I can see if there's any downstairs. The kitchen help drinks it."

"So do Americans," Ebin grinned, more at ease now that they had reached the drinking stage. "But I can make do with scotch."

Bellingham poured a dollop into two goblets and seated himself again. "All right then," he grunted. "What do you and your associates have in mind?"

"The backbone of the colonies are farmers and blacksmiths and ministers of the gospel and carpenters and shipbuilders and fishermen. A governor who actively opposes the protesters should be a man like themselves."

"Are you suggesting that the governor needs to be an American?"

"Yes, My Lord. And more. He needs to be an aristocrat."

Bellingham was all but speechless. "Shall I laugh now or later?" he rasped.

"Sir, hear me out. My associates and I believe that the governors of the colonies must be American aristocrats, and their council members as well, who, as aristocrats, may attend Parliament. In this way the present battle cry is negated."

"And that battle cry is . . . ?"

"No taxation without representation. This is the slogan all the colonies are using. None of them has accepted the stamps. In one case a stamp agent was tarred and feathered."

"Tarred and feathered!" Bellingham was appalled.

"I'm afraid so. You see, their charters specify that they may tax themselves—an internal tax, if you will. The leader of the resistance, Samuel Adams whom I have told you about, takes that to mean Parliament, being external, does not have the right to tax the colonies."

"So this man Adams does not wish to reimburse the crown for the war with France that has rid the colonists of their greatest enemy?"

"No one minds paying, my Lord. They mind being taxed by Parliament to do so."

"And they will raise the 60,000 pounds we need by taxing themselves? I doubt it."

"But if an internal tax were generated by American governors, rather than Parliament, they could do it in a more acceptable way. The colonies that produce less would pay less, the wealthier ones—ones that are involved with exports and imports, for example—would pay proportionately more."

"What sort of inducement might you offer to persuade one colony to pay more taxes than another?"

"Why, they would keep the balance of their import duties for themselves, once their share of the higher proportion has been met."

Bellingham thought about it. "Go on."

"I'll just speak for my own colony, since that is the one I know best."

"Very well. Massachusetts Bay."

"The American aristocrat governor would formulate an internal tax plan to pay for our colony's share of the 60,000 pounds, replacing the need for an external parliamentary tax."

"But this revenue would still be sent to His Majesty."

"Of course."

"And once the war debt is paid?"

"You are so clever, My Lord," fawned Worthington. "You see, the people will not necessarily know when it has been paid."

"And how would you keep this knowledge from them?"

"The clerks who account for such things would be in the pay of the government, as would the colonial treasurer. Announcing the machinations of the colonial exchequer would not be part of their duty."

"But the tax would continue?"

"Just so. The colony would still be contributing at the same rate as before, but the revenue itself would stay in Massachusetts, to pay the salaries of the governor and his councilors. And the judges, whom he would appoint. And customs collectors, whom also he would appoint."

"Positions held by you and your companions."

"Indeed," Ebin nodded.

"Hold on, Worthington!" the Earl exclaimed. "You and your companions are fabricating a fairy tale."

"Indeed we are, My Lord. But if you can see a way to help us, it can become a reality. Not only that! Once clear of the present war debt, there would be plenty of money to contribute to individuals like yourself who are instrumental in helping to put this plan in motion."

Perhaps in the form of an income stream, Bellingham thought, that would flow into his personal treasury. He was woefully lacking in cash. Most of the nobility was.

"I see your goblet is empty, as is mine," he said, putting off any answer. "Shall I refresh your drink?"

"Well, sir, since we have taken this much time to review the rudiments of the proposal, might now the butler be dispatched to the kitchen to fetch some rum?"

"If you are the one to ask him," Bellington agreed. "It would be beneath me to do so."

Ebin took no offense at this.

Encouraged by the rum when he got it—a very good brew, indeed, he asked, "Sir, what is your opinion so far?"

"Is this just a Massachusetts idea? Do any of the other colonies have similar aspirations?"

"I have yet to find that out. But my associates and I can't very well speak to them without some sort of plan that would make the idea plausible."

An American aristocracy would be a lot of work to initiate, Bellingham told himself. But an ongoing contribution to the family exchequer—that was worth whatever amount of work it required. The Earl took his time to think it over, and Ebin waited patiently, aided by the rum. When at last he spoke, Bellingham's words were a shared deliberation.

"Recently—50 years ago or so—two new Orders were created by His Majesty King George the First. Grandfather of our present monarch. One of these is the Order of the Bath, the other the Order of Westminster."

"Like the Cathedral?"

"Indeed."

"And the Bath?"

"It's a little complicated, but has to do with the medieval custom of purification before a man was elevated to knighthood."

"What do they do, these Orders?"

For the first time, Bellingham laughed. "Nothing at all. It is a matter of royal recognition. Honorary, don't you know."

"Honorary," Ebin repeated. Americans were not especially impressed with honors. Money in the bank was more to their liking.

"I'm thinking that there might be a little room in one or the other of these Orders that we could use. Given the proper incentive."

"Well, we would certainly want to contribute to their well-being, once we are in a position from which to operate," Ebin said.

Bellingham nodded his approval. "I think that would be appropriate." He rose, paced as he explored his plan. "Here is what I am thinking. The head of an Order can elevate any number of worthy men to knighthood, because he is a

baronet. Any these worthies—called Knights Companion—
are entitled to attend Parliament."

"And this would be true of an American Order, too?"

"Certainly."

"And the participating colonies would then be repre-
sented."

"Indeed. By American knights in shining armor."
Bellingham smiled, satisfied with his allusion to medieval
times.

But would it work? Ebin wondered. How did an Order
become established 3000 miles away? Would it be a sub-
sidiary of this Westminster thing-a-ma-jig? Hopefully! He
could well imagine the hoots of derision over knightly bath-
ing, should the Order of the Bath be more amenable. He
waited, breathless.

"I would need a fair amount of time, Worthington, to
arrange for so complicated and so delicate a negotiation.
And it would likely require a contribution sooner, rather
than later."

"Oh, we expected that," Ebin said lightly, though his
heart was heavy. Like any New Englander, he hated to part
with hard earned cash. "I can collect whatever amount you
suggest, sir, and bring it to you at your convenience."

"I'll notify you when I think we can actually begin this
enterprise, and let you know how much will be needed to
initiate it," the Earl said. "Meanwhile, you might contact the
appropriate leaders of the other colonies and see if they are
interested."

"I'm quite sure Rhode Island would support an American aristocracy."

"Start from that point, then. Work your way south, and I'll work here on the establishment of an American Order. Let us plan to meet again, say within a year."

"Very good, sir. My friends will be most encouraged." Rising slowly, he broached a sensitive topic. "Er . . . " He had the grace to blush. "Before we part company, may be I inquire whether or not you would know of any entertainment nearby?"

"Entertainment, eh?" The Earl chuckled. "There's a tavern in the village. Almost any sort of entertainment can be procured there." If you're willing to stoop so low, he commented to himself. Finishing his drink in one swallow, he called for his man. "A pleasure to meet you, Worthington! Look forward to your return!" Briefly shaking hands, he departed.

The unsmiling servant appeared. "This way, sir."

Indeed, Ebin thought. I think I have been dismissed. "The village," he said to the man. "I'd like to go there. Now."

"Very good, sir. I'll call the carriage."

If a satisfactory companion could be found at the tavern, his trip would be a complete success. If he liked her well enough, perhaps he could persuade her to be available when he returned, mixing pleasure with business.

The prospect was pleasing.

1767

CHAPTER TWO

Sam

Boston

Servant, he see everything, but he don't always know what he lookin at.

Slave, he see everything, he hear everything, he know everything, becuz folks forget he there. He a shadow til his Masta call.

I am slave.

I go to Dunstah Town when my Masta 12 year old. He got crippled by fallin from barn loft. His Pa buy me to carry him where he need to go. When he grow up, I carry him to carriage, to business, to his house in Boston Town. He called "Squire John Rawlings". He have brodda Tom who run famly farm in Dunstah Town, and also have a brodda Ben. Ladies, they love that boy! He have own place in Dunstah, and sometime he take me to his house, sit by fire, give me rum to drink.

I likes Masta Ben!

Masta John and me be in Boston Town when riots happen. King say: Give me money! People say: No! Not without we say so. Masta John not likin folks to say NO to King. We go back to Dunstah Town, wait til Boston quiet again.

But house filled now wid chilren. Masta Tom's poor wife die an he get a new one, Miz Betsy, who have chilren too. There be five boy chile, an one girl chile. Masta John want them go visit Miz Betsy's sistah in Boston so house be quiet.

Masta Tom not likin this. He say "NO! This is their home. And Boston has been a hornet's nest. It could be dangerous."

"You must be referring to the Stamp Tax riots."

"By God, I am. We've heard how they wrecked the governor's place."

"And hung the stamp agent in effigy," his wife say. She read newspapers. "And burnt up his carriage house."

"Plundered his wine cellar, too," say Masta Tom.

"Perhaps your sister wouldn't mind keeping the children inside until everything quiets down," say Squire. "I'll send a little money along. I've come here to Dunster for a change of atmosphere, and I'd appreciate having peace and quiet."

"Understandable," say Miz Betsy. "The past few weeks must have been hard on everyone."

"Indeed. Thank you for your understanding. I'd appreciate it, Tom, if you would try to follow your wife's example."

I see Masta Tom an Miz Betsy smile secret at each other.

Masta John say, "Send the boys to Boston, please. Have Sally go along to make sure they mind their manners." Sally be Miz Betsy's girl. 11 year old, about. "You and your wife can stay here."

"That's mighty fine of you, John," Masta Tom tell him in a voice so sweet you knowed he don't mean it at all.

Masta John and me stay in Dunstah a while, then go back to city when everthing be quiet again. We was there in April, when ship bring news. No more tax.

Everyone happy. It a warm day, everyone go outside an dance in street, an sing, an hug, an cheer. Guns fire. Flags fly from ships.

Miz Sally, she stay in Boston town with her Auntie. She think Boston mighty fine. She know how to spin—Miz Betsy teached her—an now she teach other girls how, becuz Mr. S. Adams tole them to.

Mr. S. Adams, he very important man. A lot of people listen when he say, no tax widout represent.

Then Masta John, he get married to pretty girl. Miz Elizbet. She come live in Boston house and have baby. A year go by, an afta baby big, Masta John and Miz Elizbet play dress-up and go places wid rich folk.

I drive carriage, I wear top hat, I pretend I am servant, not slave.

But I knows my place.

1768

The Order

Stanwickshire, England

"Really nice, My Lord," Ebin exclaimed. The Earl's gardens were indeed impressive, paved with cut stones, edged with smaller ones, circling around a landscaped pond. Paths led away and through plantings that were in full bloom now, in the middle of July. The Georgian houses of the colonial wealthy in Boston had gardens, to be sure, but they were much less formal—in fact, in some cases were quite wild, as befitted the countryside into which they were thrust.

In the year that he had been in America, Ebin and his friends had assessed the other colonies, set up a Loyalist newspaper in Worcester, and argued over whether the new man, Richard Awkright, should be included in their plans. In the meanwhile, the new man himself had written Lord Bellingham, further detailing his admiration for Ebin, and for the cadre of Ebin's associates.

It was Awkright who wrote the initial letter of introduction that Ebin had presented a year ago. Awkright's niece had married into Bellingham's family, and he had been introduced to the Earl at this celebratory gathering. The two of them, rather on the outside of the festivities as men are apt to be, had spent a pleasant interval in one another's company. They had kept in sporadic touch since that time, hence Awkright's initial letter.

Ebin had found Awkright willing to help fund the Loyalist newspaper and in return had championed his inclusion in the group. In consequence, Awkright had written his most recent encouraging missive.

Bellingham stopped to show his guest a bush he favored, one with truly spectacular roses on it. "Is Boston quite mellow now, with the cessation of the Stamp Tax?" he inquired.

"Everyone has been happy enough about that, indeed!" Ebin leaned over to take a sniff. "Of course, Mr. Adams wasn't pleased to note that the tax on tea remained."

"You understand why it did, of course."

"We all understand. Parliament makes it clear that it has the right to tax the colonies if it wishes."

"And has word of the new tax reached the colonies yet?"

The luster faded from the rose. Ebin stopped strolling. "New tax?"

"Chancellor of the Exchequor, Charles Townshend, is writing it even as we speak. Aside from taxing certain items—paint and paper and glass and such—it has some interesting provisions."

"Dare I ask what these might be?"

"Crown appointed commissioners who will enforce the law. To be paid by the revenues the tax generates, as well as judges and governors."

"The colonists will no longer pay these salaries out of town taxes?"

"Exactly. And in consequence the Provincial Assemblies will have no means of control over their governor or their judiciary."

"Oh, my," Ebin moaned. "I can well imagine the uproar that will stir up. Samuel Adams will be in his element."

"You're looking a little pale, old fellow," Bellingham observed. "I've arranged for your favorite beverage to be made available, once we settle down to business. Shall we get to it?" He gestured toward the mansion, and they turned, walked briskly back, through the drawing room, then into the Earl's little receiving room where a servant hovered.

On the sideboard was a blessed jug of rum, looking rather rustic among Bellingham's cut glass decanters. And yes, there was a mug, discretely hidden behind the crystal goblets. Ebin did not wait for the servant, but took the mug and the jug with him to the now-familiar couch, turned at a right angle to the hearth which held an array of ferns, as befitted the season.

The Earl shrugged away his irritation at such undisciplined behavior. "That will be all, Jones. I'll ring if I need you."

"Very good sir."

As Ebin availed himself of the rum, his anxieties ebbed away. He was here, after all, and no upheavals were going on at home because the new tax was not yet in force—perhaps not even yet discussed in Parliament. And when he concluded his business here at the Earl's castle, then there was Penelope, whom he had met at the tavern last year. He'd written her to say he was on his way back and hoped to see her soon.

Fair Penelope!

The Earl, with a snifter of brandy, seated himself on the other end of the couch. "Tell me, Worthington, have you and your associates been in contact with the appropriate leaders of the other colonies?"

"Indeed we have, sir. The New England people are very enthusiastic. The colonies in the middle are definitely interested, but wish to see details of the plan, which I told them I would have upon my return. The Southerners are interested too, but a little reluctant to align themselves too closely with us Northerners, whom they consider to be churlish."

"I can't imagine why," the Earl remarked with a straight face. "But they are interested?"

"The prospect of obtaining money interests them, I can guarantee you that. They are always in debt, and waiting for the next crop to be brought to market—"

"And a newspaper favorable to the royalists and loyalists. Has that been set up?"

"Indeed. Awkright has been helpful in that enterprise."

"Well, then, knowing this much, allow me to describe what I have learned about starting a new Order."

Ebin set himself to listen closely and carefully.

"I have conferred, many times, with the heads of both Bath and Westminster. While they see certain advantages in an American extension, their respective memberships do not."

Ebin's spirits sank.

"They don't like Americans?"

"They don't like the idea of applying for new letters patent."

"Letters patent?"

"Royal pronouncements with the force of law behind them. Like the royal governors, for instance. They are appointed by letters patent, and the peerage itself was set up using them, a long time ago."

"And the honorary Orders?"

"Yes. And to change any aspect of an Order, a new letters patent would have to be written. It is very expensive."

"How much?"

"Upward to 3000 pounds."

Yes, that was indeed expensive. Ebin helped himself to more rum.

"Now, as pertains to you and your associates. Sir Percival, head of the Westminster Order, has been exploring the possibility of an independent American Order. One that stands on its own. He points out that the head of such an Order would be able to elevate men of his choosing to the rank of Knights Companion, who would form his council."

"You mean, he can dub them himself even though he is an American?"

"He can, once he has become a baronet. And any one of his Knights Companion can represent his colony in the House of Commons—which, I believe, is a major sticking point?"

"No taxation without representation, yes."

"You see, then, once an American Order is established, representation will be a moot point. Your Mr. Adams will no longer have anything to complain about."

"I'll be damned!" exclaimed Ebin.

"And Sir Percival himself is agreeable to approaching His Majesty with the idea."

"His Majesty!"

"Naturally. Only the king can create the Order by writing the letters patent. And once he has been made aware of the advantages—political and financial—he most likely will agree to it."

"This gentleman, Sir what-his-name, is really helpful, isn't he!"

Bellingham drew back, as though an offensive smell had entered the room.

"Never do that!" he scowled.

"Do what?"

"If you can't recall the name of a highly ranked person, then use an acceptable alternative. In this case, you might have said, 'the gentleman you mentioned.'"

"Sorry about that."

"I tell you this because in the presence of Sir Percival or any other member of the peerage, you would not be included in any subsequent conversation were you to say such a demeaning thing."

"Touchy bastards, eh?" The rum was having its desired effect.

"Let us return to the matter at hand," the Earl sniffed. "We also decided that we'd suggest the name for the new Order so His Majesty won't need to trouble himself."

"Yes?"

"Capitalizing on the oldest power in known history . . ."

"Yes? yes?"

"Oligarchy, dear fellow. Rule by the richest. The head of the Order will be the Supreme Oligarch, who will be the royal governor. The Knights Companion will be the Lesser Oligarchs. They will serve on the Governor's council and elect, from among themselves, representatives to Parliament. And there will be Least Oligarchs who will see to it that Loyalists are favored in your various town meetings and in your Provincial Assembly."

"I'm overwhelmed," Ebin breathed. "It's perfect, sir!"

"Yes, it is, rather." Bellingham raised his glass and looked through it at the sun pouring through the window of his study. A rich, satisfying, ruby red. He was suffused with satisfaction. Solutions to puzzles were always gratifying.

"There is still nothing in writing, is there?" Ebin asked. Upper Crust people seemed always to keep memoranda about events important or interesting to them.

"We have kept no notes of our discussions. Tell me: who might you have in mind to be Supreme Oligarch, if I may ask?"

"Why, myself," Worthington smiled.

The Earl did his best to maintain an air of neutrality. "Do you believe others of your compatriots would agree?"

"Well, it may take a while to settle the matter. They are accustomed to my leadership, but your friend, Awkright, thinks he would do a fine job himself."

"Ah. So he has decided to join you."

"We have allowed him to join us, sir," Ebin informed him.

"I see." Awkright had style. Breeding, as far as any Yankee had any. A far better choice than Worthington,

Bellingham thought, but he guessed style and breeding were not of importance in America. He sighed. "Describe the articles in your Loyalist newspaper, if you please."

"The editorials praise His Majesty's wisdom and intelligence. He is, I understand, very interested in science and horticulture. Other articles discuss his concern for his American subjects, defending them such that his war debts are greatly enlarged. His distress over the Boston resistance. His pride in his loyal subjects."

"Ah." The Earl nodded in satisfaction. "Splendid. And you have contacted the gentlemen from other colonies, is that right?"

"To the extent of sending them copies of our editorials, along with a note to each, yes, we have. We didn't want to do more, for fear of appearing to be overanxious."

"Now that you know how the Order will be set up, I suggest you actually visit these individuals. You can describe how the baronet of the Massachusetts Order will elevate men to knighthood, thus resolving the representation problem, and you can explain that, in time, the other colonies can set up Orders of their own in a similar fashion."

"We shall, My Lord."

"And get that newspaper to begin publishing articals that praise the Tory businessmen and the contributions they make to the cities in which they live, like Baltimore and New York and Philadelphia. Make them seem like heroes."

"The Quakers control Philadelphia. They'd probably be upset if we gave the Tories too much credit."

"A little controversy is good for circulation. And you must raise more funds The thousand pounds you brought only wets the whistle."

"It takes time to liquidate assets, My Lord. We had to work hard for that much."

"Work harder. I'd suggest 5000 for each of the men who helps bring the Oligarchy into reality."

"Three."

"Four."

"Three and a half."

"Very well."

They drank to it while Ebin tried to calculate how long it would take and how much the final total would be. Oh, well, he thought. No pain, no gain.

"Ollie Garky?" he asked. "Is that what it's called?"

"That's what it sounds like. I'll write it out for you."

"That would be helpful, My Lord." Ebin bowed humbly, and waited until he could manage dismissal.

Outside the drawing room door hovered the man-servant. "A conveyance to the village, if you please."

The man nodded, and Ebin congratulated himself on sounding much like the Earl. Keep this up, he told himself, and he would be a fit aristocrat!

But first, the fair Penelope.

He hoped.

CHAPTER FOUR

Margaret

I was just a girl when I met the man who would one day be my husband.

Tyler Moore.

My father had sent me to the print shop where Tyler worked. It was my first assignment: to submit an order for a poster advertising our company's latest imports.

He was busy, and so angry and upset that he appeared not to notice me. The British had returned Fortress Louisbourg to France and Tyler's brother had died in the taking of it two years earlier, in 1746. Many of our boys had died up there at Isle Royale, north of Nova Scotia. Tyler wasn't the only angry person in New England that day, I assure you!

My father's poster being my first assignment, I waited patiently.

Our company was called Roberge Imports. My father was of Huguenot descent. His great-grandfather had emigrated from France when the Protestants were under siege there. The British had offered them asylum, and some had gone to Ireland, taking their knowledge of weaving with them. That is how we came to be importers of Irish damask and linen, as well as British brocades and velvets.

I have worked all my life to further the interests of our family's business. I gave up the man I loved, and when Tyler and I married, I bound him to a prenuptial agreement that would guarantee my retaining control of Roberge Imports. It was an arrangement that superseded coverture (which means that all your assets automatically belong to your spouse, by the way).

Tyler understood how important this control was to me, and did not baulk.

Oh? You wish to learn about the man I loved?

Very well. That happened when I was stranded at Fortress Louisbourg, after it had been returned to the French.

Stranded, you exclaim.

Yes, quite literally.

I was seventeen years old and on my way to London with my mother, to meet Roberge agents there. But a storm hit us and the ship foundered. My mother and everyone else was swept away—everyone but me. I was rescued by a French schooner out of Louisbourg, and was taken there to arrange my return home.

I have not mentioned that, being of Huguenot descent, I speak French, which was most fortunate as there I was, among French speaking people who hated the Americans and the English indiscriminately. Because I spoke their language, I was able to hide the fact that I was of the enemy, and though prostrate at losing my mother, I managed to cooperate with a roundabout plan to get me back home.

This plan was carried out by a man of mixed English and Indian blood. Such people—we call them half-breeds—are disdained by us British—but during our travels through Nova Scotia I learned that beneath his anger and determination to avenge his people, Marc Duval was a sensitive, principled, and very attractive man.

We became close—very close—but there was no hope for us. We were forced to part.

Broken-hearted, I married Tyler Moore a year later. By then he owned the print shop, due to the timely death of the gentleman to whom he had been indentured. My father never really recovered from the death of my mother and could not operate Roberge Imports himself, but since it was mine by prenuptial agreement, I took it over.

We adopted an Acadian boy that I'd found in New Towne, where a few Acadian families had been placed for the duration of the war. Anton Dupres. No father. No mother. All of the Acadians in Nova Scotia had been expelled from their lands and dispersed throughout the colonies. Anton's parents probably got put on a different ship than he did, and God-only knew where they might have ended up. The family caring for Anton was strained just meeting the needs of their own children, and gratefully gave him to us.

He was a darling, and we both loved him. He was eight years old, bright and capable. We taught him English and his numbers, and when he was old enough, Tyler began teaching him to run the press at the print shop.

By 1765, when the Stamp Tax was visited upon us, we had two children of our own, Janelle, 6, and Charles, 4, and

I was pregnant again. We were living in my family's house, my father having passed away soon after my marriage. Tyler ran the shop, I ran Roberge Imports, while our cook and our family's nursemaid cared for Janelle and Charles during the day. At night, when I came home, I taught the children French. If the day ever came that Janelle wanted independence, I would cede the company to her. Otherwise, Charles would take it into the future.

Tyler was calm and supportive of me, but the tax issue was another story. I'm sure you can understand why I was unimpressed by a boycott on British imports, since my entire business depended on them. The boycott was Sam Adams' idea, and Tyler was very loyal to him.

Adams first promoted non-importation in 1763, right after the so-called "French and Indian War". Parliament revised and renamed an old import duty as a start in paying the war debt. No one was awfully alarmed by the Sugar Tax, which was small, and we business people went right on importing.

But only two years later, when that damned Stamp Tax was made law, Tyler could print nothing without buying a stamp to affix onto it. No advertisements, no broadsides, no newspaper articles, and in protest he shut up his shop, joining the local Sons of Liberty. They used their time trying to convince everyone not to buy British until the merchants of London put enough pressure on Parliament to annul the tax.

Since it affected my husband so directly, I imported nothing. But I did not close my shop. I'd bought a lot of

French goods after the war was over, and stored them in the attic of our house and both shops, so I could stay open selling only the imports I already had on hand.

Tyler would have liked me to close, I know, but the decision to remain open was mine alone. You wonder why I was so stubborn about this? You may not understand how unusual it was for a woman to control her own destiny! Of course, at home my husband was lord and master, and I was careful not to transgress there. And while he was not happy that Roberge Imports remained open, he could do nothing about it.

My Tyler believed, as did Mr. Adams, that Parliament did not have the right to tax us. I have privately suspected that at the heart of the matter, Adams wanted the colonies to separate from the mother country, yet I said nothing of this to Tyler. Like most Americans, he was a King's man. His objections were to Parliament, not His Majesty. He attributed the same loyalty to Adams, who cleverly concealed his true intent.

But as I've mentioned, Tyler's older brother had died when we captured Fort Louisbourg from the French—the one the English gave it back.

And before that betrayal, Tyler's father had been ruined by a Parliamentary decision that terminated Boston's Land Bank, just as had Mr. Adam's father. The London merchants had put pressure on Parliament to close the bank because if the colonies could produce their own money, they needn't borrow from those merchants, and the loss of interest generated from their loans was, I gather, substantial.

Which is why Sam Adams believed the merchants were the strongest ally (or enemy) you could have.

In 1765 no stamp was ever affixed to anything. Boston's allotment was stored at Castle William, and left there to rot. Within a year the day was won; trade could resume again. Only a small tax on tea remained ...

Our new baby was born by then—Steven—so now we were free of strife over taxes and could live in peace with our growing family. Our businesses thrived. Anton grew tall and strong and loved working with Tyler at the print shop.

Then Chancellor of the Exchequer, Charles Townshend, devised a new tax, and had commissioners appointed to enforce it. The question of non-importation arose again.

With each successive attempt of Parliament to raise money from the colonies, more and more sea-ports and cities adopted boycott as a means to force repeal. More and more British merchants were vocal in our support lest they be forced into bankruptcy.

So, as you might expect, in view of the new tax, the Sons of Liberty girded their loins and plotted. In October of 1768 the first three of the five Customs Commissioners for Boston arrived. A Guy Fawkes Day parade was in progress, which we loyal British subjects held every October 9th. This year, however, it was subtly commandeered by the Sons who somehow diverted it to the waterfront just as the commissioners were disembarking.

Peaceful, although loud, a thousand men and women accompanied the newcomers to their recently constructed offices. The crowd carried the traditional effigies of Guy Fawkes and the Pope. But this year there was an additional one—that of Charles Townshend, and well, yes, the Commissioners got nervous when Champaign Charlie ended up in a bonfire. Very nervous.

They petitioned Parliament for armed support, which seemed a little overly dramatic, I thought, but I was so preoccupied by fighting with Tyler that I paid the whole matter little attention.

"You don't understand, Meg! Just listen," Tyler urged. "The Townshend Acts are about more than taxes. It's about who's in control. The governor, the council, and the judges—under this Act all of them will be paid by the crown. And the Governor will appoint the council, instead of their being elected by the House of Representatives in our Provincial Assembly. Our charters will be worthless. Don't you understand?"

I suppose I did understand, but if I joined the protest by not selling British goods, I was out of business. Tyler would be out of business too (because got his paper from England, and his ink) and . . .

What were we supposed to live on? I asked.

Apparently the Sons of Liberty thought we could manage. It being autumn, we could lay away stocks of root vegetables and apples and rum. Homespun goods which were rough, perhaps, but perfectly serviceable, would be substituted for English cloth. We could make our own tea out of leaves or berries. Tyler thought it would work.

I didn't care if it would work or not. I couldn't wear homespun and run a store full of Irish damask and English velvet. My customers were mostly upper class people who were certainly Tories, and would not regard me kindly if I advertised a connection with the rebels, which a homespun dress would do. I stood my ground and refused to close.

He left me. Just moved out, into the attic of his print shop which no longer stored French laces and wine because I'd sold them all. Strictly temporary, he said. He led a group of Adams' followers, and felt he couldn't live with me and lead them at the same time. I did not bother to mention that perhaps I didn't consider it a temporary arrangement. There was no point making a bad situation worse.

His men picketed Roberge Imports. Signs were plastered on my windows, urging everyone to avoid doing business with me. But my clientelle were the women of the Better Sort. They came accompanied by their husbands or brothers or gentlemen cousins. I think the men were happy to provide protection, as there was almost nothing a Loyalist could do to show his disapproval of Sam Adams and the boycott except to buy British.

Then His Majesty's troops arrived in response to the commissioners' request for help. Two regiments from Halifax, Nova Scotia. With bayonets on their rifles and their officers carrying drawn swords, they entered the city and set up their headquarters on the Common and marched around Boston and made sure order was had.

Roberge Imports was no longer picketed. Soldiers scraped off the signs pasted on my windows by the Sons of Liberty. Although Anton would have dearly liked to be one of the Sons, Tyler forbade it. They did some illegal things like breaking windows or setting small fires on the front steps of Tory businesses—all at night, of course, and it was too risky for a boy.

Instead, Anton would help me in the store where he'd be out of the way of trouble.

The boy sulked most of the time, taking forever to do what was asked of him until Tyler intervened. I deserved respect, he said. I had made Anton's life in America possible, and whether he agreed with my decisions or even my politics or not, he must behave politely and do the jobs he was assigned. Or else . . .

Tyler came to the house every evening, to attend to our children, check in with Anton and me—but he wouldn't stay. "We are at war, Margaret," he said. "I don't want to compromise you, and I don't want to compromise myself. I can't see another alternative. I miss you, dearest. I wish it weren't this way."

Soon enough I became accustomed to our separation. The autumn weather became brisk. Then, as the extreme cold approached, I closed the shop as I always did in the dead of winter because it was so difficult to heat. Charles was old enough to go to school, but we didn't want him on the street with a lot of soldiers about. I tutored him and Janelle and some neighborhood children, teaching them to write their letters and numbers and learn the alphabet. Finally winter was done, and with Anton's help, I opened the shop up again.

The ladies flocked through my doors to select their summertime fabrics. Business was wonderful, but my inventory was getting low and I worried about ordering more and unloading it here in Boston where the Sons of Liberty might destroy it. Could I secure protection for it? Did I dare? Yes. I dared. After all, I was loyal to His Majesty, was I not? Did I not deserve the protection of his troops not only at my store, but at the waterfront? The British Commander assured me that, indeed, when the time came, they'd be on the lookout for a ship, and would even unload my goods for me.

It worked. I ordered, the goods arrived, and the soldiers even put the fabrics in the shop's attic for me, since Anton refused to do so out of loyalty to Tyler.

Tyler and I were at sword's points by then, for I had not concealed my Loyalist sympathies from him. We maintained a polite façade in front of the servants and children and managed to speak civilly when we had to. Summer passed. Fall crept in, and then winter, and again I closed the shop, avoided Tyler when he came acalling, nurtured my children and tutored them and the neighboring little ones as winter moved into the January thaw, and then February when the sky was lighter at dawn, and then it was March.

We prepared to reopen Roberge Imports; Anton lit the stoves and we brought the new shipment of linens and damask and brocades in the shop's attic downstairs and went through them, setting up our displays. We worked hard, dusting and washing windows and restocking shelves, and were sleeping deeply from the unaccustomed exertion the night Tyler burst in, dragging me from my slumber. Little Steven, sleeping beside me, stirred, then settled.

"Meg! Meg!" Tyler shook me. Quite hard.

Outside, on Hanover Street, footsteps pounded past.

Instantly I was wide awake.

"There's been a shooting," he said, quietly as he could. "I think one of the soldiers fired at someone, down town. I'm going to find out. Whatever happens, stay inside. I'll come back as soon as I can and tell you everything."

I promised I would stay inside.

He ran out to join the crowd.

There were more shots. More men went by. Armed.

A church bell began to ring.

Then another and another.

We were under attack.

1770

CHAPTER FIVE

The Negotiators

Stanwickshire, England

"**M**r. Worthington, sir! You must feel like a mariner rather than a merchant! Surely you've spent more time on the sea than off it, these past two years!"

Ebin's smile was polite. "Indeed, My Lord."

He had come back twelve months ago with half of the monetary enhancements he'd agreed to. The rest would come soon, he'd assured the Earl.

When he told the fellows about being Ollie Garks, they could hardly contain themselves. Many of the Tories in the other colonies had been excited by the plan, too, even the Southerners. The newspaper had reported the deeds of Tory leaders in their respective communities, gratifying the local Loyalists. And to top it all off, he had negotiated further advantages for himself. After he'd bid the Earl farewell, when he was last in England, he'd hastened to the village, to the tavern, and to Penelope.

Again she was waiting.

"But I'm glad you wrote me that you were coming, sir," she giggled. "So I was certain to be free."

He was not sure exactly what she might be free from, and wisely did not ask.

She had hired a private room at the village inn, across the street from the tavern, and while not a lush accommodation, at least it was theirs for as long as they wished. Lolling on the generously sized bed, to which they had hastened, she allowed a breast to peek above the quilt as she played with the hair on his chest.

"Do you think we might go for a carriage ride whilst you are here?" She kissed him gently and brought his hand up.

Ah, her breast was so soft, so full! The kiss became deeper.

He had stayed a week, taken her for rides every day, and wondered what it would be like if she came to America to live. Near him, but far enough away so that his wife would never know . . .

He returned to Boston, to the Loyalist newspaper, to the endless task of getting more money, to looking for a place in which he might establish Penelope . . .

But then came the shooting.

The Earl, knowing Ebin fairly well by now, spoke to his man-servant.

"The gentleman would enjoy rum," he directed, and the servant quickly brought the jug and the mug to the guest. Ebin, unhappy, even morose, poured himself a generous portion and sighed.

Patiently, the Earl waited.

"You have probably not yet heard about the most recent lamentable event in Boston."

"No, I have not."

"I regret to tell you, sir, that His Majesty's soldiers shot some civilians."

"Soldiers shot people? Shot them dead?"

"Three on the spot. Two more died some time later."

"Five people dead." The Earl thought about the ramifications of this new information. "Were they armed, these citizens? Did they threaten the soldiers?"

"A boy taunted a guard at the Customs House. Threw a snowball."

"I can't believe this, Worthington!"

Ebin was unable to believe it, himself, and took a long swallow of rum. He struggled on.

"There were barracks nearby and the guard called for help. Some more soldiers appeared and some residents, hearing the commotion, came running and there was more shouting and one of the soldiers fired. Then another. Then a few more. The church bells began to ring and the whole town turned out—bells generally mean fire, sir."

"Go on, man!" The Earl was not interested in this detail.

"There were more than a hundred people, milling about," Ebin explained, "because of the bells. Many had heard the shots, so they were armed."

"Good grief! Do you think they might have taken on the soldiers, if the circumstances had allowed?"

"Well, there were a lot more armed civilians than there were soldiers at the Customs House, sir. But the rest of the regiment was just up the street, in their barracks. We're lucky it didn't come to that."

The Earl sighed deeply. "And here we thought a regiment or two would keep the peace," he grumbled. "Looks like we were wrong. How did it all end?"

"The soldiers will be bivouacked at Castle William Island from now on—the offenders are in jail and will be tried for murder. The people seem satisfied. Public funerals were going on as I was leaving, with huge numbers mourners following the caskets to the cemetery."

"Surely these demonstrations kept everyone stirred up?"

"Indeed, sir. I believe that was the point. Can you guess who orchestrated them?"

"Bah!" Restless, the Earl got to his feet and began to pace. "By now word surely has reached the colonies that the taxes have been rescinded."

"Repealed!" After so much worry, so much anxiety over the heavy hand of the military! Ebin swore. "The whole debacle could have been avoided if we'd known the taxes were about to be repealed."

"Most likely the uproar has settled down by now," Bellingham soothed. "The people have short memories."

Companionably, they drank until the Earl thought his guest was steady and ready.

"I must tell you that I have encountered an intractable problem that must be resolved before we can move forward with our plan."

"Oh?" The plan. Yes. That was his purpose in being here, was it not? With the help of the rum, Ebin threw off the troubles at home. An intractable problem. That had an ominous tone to it. But, he told himself, founding an American aristocracy—or any other, really—was not a simple matter. There would always be details requiring attention, if not outright warfare.

"I thought the negotiations were going well. But recently it seems resistence has arisen to Americans having titles similar to those of the British peerage."

"Really!" Worthington was astounded. "Even the baronets?" The lowest in the pecking order, and not really part of the peerage at all.

"Consider it for a moment. Titles go back to medieval times, and a new Order with new titles can never be seen as equivalent."

"Well, certainly that point can't be argued," said Ebin, trying to be nice about it. "We can't become old."

"Sir Percival has suggested that an entirely new Order could engender the same respect as Westminster's as long as it occupies a lower position than Westminster or Bath."

"Below the bottom-most?"

The Earl motioned downward with both hands, calming the distress he saw arising. "So no one would feel threatened."

"Who would feel threatened? Please explain." Worthington was intensely annoyed. "People like you? You have land. You have country estates. You dress as we do, your women have jewels and set a superlative table.

The same can be said of our upper class gentry. Is that why we pose a threat, sir?" Ebin could not keep the sneering note out of his voice no matter how hard he tried. "Because we're as good as you are?"

Offended, the Earl drew a deep breath and consulted his brandy. "Let us not squabble. I have told you what the problem is, and Sir Percival has come up with a solution to it. Are you ready to listen?"

"Go on," Ebin sulked.

"If the new—lower—Order will have limits on its membership, it will not be able to expand unduly and overtake us."

"Overtake! Really, My Lord, this is not to be believed."

The Earl paid no heed. "Others with whom we have spoken believe it would work."

"Others?"

"I introduced you to them a year ago."

"Ah. Those others." The ones for whom he was working his bottom off, to pay for their support of the incipient Oligarchy.

"Men who think your idea of proportionate taxation is a stroke of genius. His Majesty approves of the plan, by the way, as long as the elevation of your leader will be done privately."

"Of course. We would never presume otherwise."

"And the numbers are kept constant. 10 Lesser. 15 Least."

"I'd have to consult my associates. I can't dictate to them."

"Then, shall we arrange for the letters patent?"

"How much?" asked Ebin wearily.

"We can get it done for two thousand pounds."

"It will take a while for us to raise it. And we're still behind on our pledged amount."

"Sir Percival and I will take it out of the contributions you've already made."

A large burden lifted itself from his shoulders. It would be easier to talk the fellows into being the lowest of the low if they didn't have to pay extra for the privilege.

"We can have medals, can't we?" he asked, somewhat belligerently.

"Indeed. When you and your associates have paid everything you promised us, we'll get them cast."

"Is it appropriate that our wives make us sashes? And can they make sashes for themselves? It would make them happy, Your Lordship." Sashes would soften the blow when the women learned how low they really were, Ebin guessed.

"Why don't you let me take care of that detail when everything is ready," said the Earl. "I'll have them especially emblazoned, so they can't be duplicated by anyone pretending to be you."

"A good point," Ebin concurred. "Otherwise everyone will be dubbing everyone else and the whole lot wearing sashes."

"Indeed," Bellingham said without even a quiver at the thought. "Do you continue to publish articles about Tory businessmen?"

"Yes, sir."

"And the Philadelphia Quakers?"

"Did not dignify our praise with so much as a fart in our direction."

"Ah," remarked Bellington.

"In the meantime my associates have directed me to take a look at the revenues actually generated by import duties so that we can be ready to start paying whatever tribute we agree on, you and I, to whomever you think should get it, besides whatever is due His Majesty—once the take-over is complete."

"And for yourselves?"

"Whatever is left, sir. Whatever is left. And if it is insufficient, raise the tax a little more. The people won't even notice."

Worthington had forgotten all about the dead citizens shot by His Majesty's military, the Earl noted with relief. And with only a little tax on tea left, most likely everything would be quiet for a while.

"Well, then, if you are in no hurry to return, Worthington, I have arranged dinners with the appropriate men and we can discuss those tributes."

"I'm more than willing! This evening, however, I am already spoken for." Ebin could not help smiling.

"Hmmmmm," Bellington observed. "Tomorrow, then."

"You didn't give me much warning," Penelope complained. "I haven't prepared properly for your arrival."

She looked pretty well prepared, Ebin thought, but knew a little groveling was in order. "As long as you are here, my dear, that is enough. More than enough."

"Did you miss me?"

"I always miss you."

"Well, darling, I have a suggestion to make. It will take care of all our problems. My being here—or not. Your missing me. My missing you."

"That would be nice," he murmured, his lips nibbling at her lovely body as she lay there disheveled and wanton and altogether desirable.

"You could bring me to Boston," she purred. "Then you would always know where I am."

It would not do to tell her he had already looked into this possibility. "And where would you stay, in Boston." His voice was muffled as he made his way further down.

"Someplace you would provide. Some place secret."

He had by then found her very own secret place, and did not answer.

"Can you—will you—do that?" she panted.

"Ummmmm," he replied.

There was no hurry to go home. When he did reach Boston, he would spend more time looking for suitable quarters for Penelope. He'd talk the fellows around to this ridiculous requirement of reduced rank, and they'd all pool their information on sources of money. Often it turned out that one or the other of them had overlooked a possibility that someone else had found profitable. In a year or two they'd be able to pay off their pledges. Once it began to look as though the dubbing would happen, they'd hold an election for Supreme Oligarch. Who would, of course,

be himself. Come back to England and be dubbed. Collect
the sashes, the medals, the letters what-ever-they-were and
return to Massachusetts. Establish himself as royal governor, then begin the task of initiating Boston and then the
colony to government by Oligarchy, dangling representation
in Parliament in front of anyone who might be doubtful.

It was going to happen!

He would make it happen!

CHAPTER SIX

Elizabeth

My life in America reads like a ladies novel.

Chapter One: English girl flees to Boston. I didn't know there was going to be political turmoil nearly as soon as I arrived. Nor did I care, because soon after I got there, I discovered . . .

. . . I was pregnant, the result of my troubles in England.

So begins chapter two: English girl marries her benefactor, Squire John Rawlings. He was an older man in business, crippled from a fall when he was young. He agreed to give my unborn baby his name in exchange for my pretending to be of noble lineage. I had been employed by an aristocratic lady in England, and all I had to do was mimic her. John was sure this would enable us to become part of the Trinity Crowd, Boston's more elite citizenry, and he very much wanted to belong to it.

There is a footnote to this chapter. I fell in love with Squire John's brother, Ben, nearly as soon as I met him. He was a follower of Samuel Adams of Boston, who protested a new law that was enacted just then. So naturally Ben opposed it, too, and had to leave town on an errand for

Adams just as I was learning to trust him. He left in a hurry, without telling me when he'd be back.

Which is bad enough, but it was just then that I realized I was pregnant.

So I married John quickly. We moved into his Boston house to await the baby, and the third chapter of my life's book began.

After Paul's birth, we were free to move forward. I was to become Lady Lisabet Hopewell, an empty headed, cheerful party-goer recently arrived from Philadelphia where the aristocratic Hopewells were said to congregate when visiting the New World. My task was acceptance of John and Lady Lisabet by the Trinity Crowd.

They were wealthy Anglicans, Loyalists one and all, wanting nothing more than to be recognized as a kind of aristocracy by His Majesty, and so having a member of the nobility in their midst made them very happy. Our scheme was going well until a year and a half later when my baby Paul was kidnapped.

I say this calmly enough now, but I was far from calm at the time! In the course of my pretending to be an aristocrat, I had the misfortune of meeting Lord Harry Ashline, the brother of the man in England who had raped me—Paul's real father. They were the sons of the Lady to whom I was secretary, and Lord Harry, the younger, had become an officer in His Majesty's army. He came to Boston with his regiment in order to enforce compliance with another new tax that would be more heavily enforced than the last one.

Between them, Lord Harry and my husband contrived to kidnap Paul, planning to take him to England to Harry's brother, who, unable to produce more children, would be overjoyed to learn he had a male heir. Made legitimate by a newly discovered marriage certificate. My husband was sure that Lord Harry and his brother could get him a baronetcy in exchange for my child.

They had not counted on Ben.

The youngest Rawlings brother—the one who wasn't there when I needed him. He was at my side now, though, our misunderstanding having been cleared up, and with his connection to the Sons of Liberty, he was able to find Paul, and get us both away from Boston before John and Lord Harry could stop us.

We went to Philadelphia, Ben and Paul and I, and found a place to live in the north part of the city. Ben became a carpenter, I learned how to weave, and in due time, Paul was joined by a little sister—Annie. Frequently Ben went up to Boston to help Tyler Moore's Sons of Liberty. This particular group was not averse to breaking windows and setting fire to businesses that didn't support the non-importation agreement. Samuel Adams, of course, would not have countenanced such things, but Tyler was careful to hide the facts from him.

We heard about the Boston massacre nearly as soon as it happened, and then we learned the troops had been removed to Castle William Island and the shooters would be tried for their lives later in the year. We heard about mob-attended funeral processions for the murdered citizens of Boston, and then we learned the Townshend Tax had been repealed.

With only a tax on tea left, and the troops gone, everyone was complacent. The trial of the soldiers interested folks for a while. After that, nothing. Samuel Adams' followers wilted and fell away. He carried on alone with his quill and inkpot, outlining and summarizing the events surrounding all the revenue acts, knitting them together in a sequence that showed how the colonists' rights were being lost. His articles were published not only in Boston but everywhere else, too. But that was all he could do. Write. And write. And write.

Boston was tranquil.

New York went about its business as usual.

Quaker quiet fell on Philadelphia—and then Ben got word of his brother John's death.

We packed up our things and with Paul and Annie boarded the stage to Providence, then took another to Dunster where the Rawlings family lived.

We barely made it to the funeral. Leaving our baggage on the porch of the Dunster Tavern, we hastened, travel-stained and staggering with fatigue, to the burial already underway.

The townsmen and women opened a path, at the far end of which was Ben's brother Tom and his expanded family. They greeted us silently, Tom's wife Betsy hugging me and her daughter, Sally, gently relieving Ben of

Annie, who having been awake and cranky all during our travels, fell fast asleep in her arms. The younger members of the family opened a place for Paul while the minister continued reading the usual Bible passages and everyone else bowed their heads again, now that our presence was ascertained.

I did not bow mine. I looked at John's coffin, and the dirt piled up that would cover the final resting place of my less-than-beloved husband. He had done me great favors and great injuries.

On the far edge of the gathered mourners was the slave, Sam. I knew John had planned to manumit him, but the end was quick and somewhat unexpected—a catarrh one day, pneumonia the next with a fever so high that he may not have even thought of freeing Sam. No matter. Surely Tom, who stood to inherit everything, would attend to it.

After the service we walked back to the Rawlings place—a farm house made over into a Georgian-looking mansion, with pillars and a paladian window over the front door and four chimneys, two on each side. The place looked truly grand; John's and my Trinity friends had loved it. Soon enough, I was to discover, they'd have the pleasure of lounging in its opulence once again.

Tom and Betsy had cleared out John's downstairs chamber for our use. The last time we here, Ben and I had stolen into it clandestinely—a memory he, too, was recalling, judging from his not-quite concealed smirk. We were ushered in by Sally, who was still carrying Annie, sleeping peacefully.

"Making up for last night," Ben grimaced. "Lillybet (his favorite name for me)—would you like to rest? You haven't slept much."

Indeed I had not. I'd been dandling Annie in the coach so my men could sleep.

"Yes, please," I sighed, and sank gratefully onto the feather mattress, all puffed up and inviting, burrowed into an equally soft pillow, held out my arms for my little daughter, made sure she was safe beside me and closed my eyes, welcoming sleep as a parched wanderer welcomes a spring of blessedly cool water—

To no avail.

I heard Ben and Sally enter the keeping room, which is just behind the chamber, with the borning room sandwiched in between. Its door must have been ajar, for I could hear every word spoken.

Tom was there, of course, and his wife (Sally's mother, Betsy). Two men must have come in through the keeping room (since I'd have heard them if they came in the front). Ben introduced them to his brother.

"Tom, this is my friend Tyler Moore, from Boston, and Anton Dupre, his . . . his . . . "

"Helper," said Anton Dupre.

"Right-hand man," said Tyler Moore. "We brought your stuff from the Inn, by the way."

Ben thanked them, then ascertained the location of Paul (still with the other children, all of them presently playing in the nearby barn). Betsy found some rum. Murmurings and scufflings went on as the men seated themselves and passed the jug around. Sally made tea for her mother and herself.

"Ben and Anton and I have been working together in Boston for quite a while," I heard Tyler say after some time had passed, the weather had been dissected, John's demise respectfully noted. "I hope you're up to hearing what I want to tell you. If not, we can come back tomorrow morning. We can take a room at the Inn."

"I guess you want to talk about the Sons of Liberty," Tom said.

"In fact, we do."

"Ben has never made a secret of his admiration for Sam Adams. At lot of fellows around here consider themselves followers too, thanks to him."

"Is that going to be an embarrassment for you?" Ben asked. "Now that you're the Squire?"

"Not me," said Tom.

His wife Betsy disagreed. "We've always been a little uncomfortable with John's pretentions. Elizabeth's too, if you want to know."

"Lillybet did what she had to do, to keep John happy," Ben said quickly.

"She looked like she was enjoying herself."

"I expect she was," Ben agreed, "when she could pretend she was on stage, like in a theater."

"What's a theater?" Sally asked. There were none in Boston, or in Massachusetts, for that matter, because the founding fathers, being Puritan, disapproved of such frivolity.

Some time was spent explaining this phenomenon. Tom brought them back to the task at hand. "You're here for a reason, Mr. Moore. I'd like to hear what it is." Tyler Moore explained. "We've suspected for a while that the Boston Tories are hatching some plan or another that will work to their advantage. They've been raising a lot of money for the past few years, and we can't figure out where it's going. We think we'd better find out, if we can. Everyone is content, just now, with the Townshend taxes repealed and all. We think these Tories will see it as a good time to put their scheme—whatever it is—in place."

"And why are you telling me about this?"

"Because we might need to use this house again."

"Like before?" Tom asked. "When Elizabeth was so high and mighty?"

"Yes. It's the Boston Tories—the Trinity Crowd—that believe Elizabeth is nobility, and it's them that think this house is part of a grand estate. We believe they'd like to come back for a visit, especially if Lady Lisabet invites them."

"Lady Lisabet."

"John's wife."

"Still is, you know."

"We'll fix that as soon as we can. Right now we need to get Lady Lisabet re-established, renewing her old friendships and proposing that the Trinity Crowd come to visit. She might remind them that the dining room is a wonderful place for the men to have a meeting. Far from Boston where they might be overheard by inquisitive and talkative servants."

"And?"

Tyler smiled. "I'm told that the dining room is adjacent to a hall closet, built so that a person inside can hear everything being said."

"The front hall closet, do you mean?"

"You didn't know about that?"

"No."

"I'd be glad to show you," Ben offered.

Tom deflected this invitation. "I've got to piss," he growled. Scrapings came next as a bench was moved to allow his egress.

There was silence while everyone in the kitchen waited for him to return, however long that would take. They had everything planned, from the sound of it, including my part in it. I smiled to myself. As silly as she was, I'd enjoy watching Lady Lisabet's antics again. But I could not think long about her just then, because within the waiting silence, I disappeared, joining my little Annie in slumber.

CHAPTER SEVEN

Tom

Our life was pleasant enough, Betsy's and mine. The house had been made over and had fireplaces in every room, which was a blessing in winter! Sometimes John and his wife, Elizabeth, invited their Tory friends to spend time here. Upon those occasions we camped out in the barn, Betsy, the children, and me, so that their friends would believe the place was exclusively John's, as would be expected of a wealthy couple.

When they weren't in Dunster, Betsy and I had the place to ourselves and our shared brood of little ones.

She had agreed to marry me, after my dear wife died, if I would give her privacy and respect it. We could still enjoy time together, like walking by the river or attending a gathering at the house of mutual friends. She liked me well enough, she said, but wanted no more children. So we got married and I found an out-of-the house resolution to the problem of separate sleeping arrangements. With Betsy's blessing, I might add.

We lived as peacefully as possible with seven offspring in the house, until Elizabeth left my brother, John, and he came back from Boston, apparently planning to stay forever.

He took over the whole front of the house, and we all settled in again, our lives went on much as they had before.

Except for avoiding John all we could. Being deserted by Elizabeth was too much for him, and he became nastier every day. I felt damn sorry for his slave, Sam, and more than once interrupted the abuse coming out of John's mouth when the slave displeased him. (Sam was smart enough to stand three feet away when that was going on.)

Then the Townshend taxes were lifted, except for the levy on tea. Everything got peaceful again, except the weekly articles that Sam Adams wrote about how our liberties were slowly being lost. My friends and I debated these at the Dunster Tavern. After all, that is what the tavern is for—a comradely place where men can talk about the issues of the day without getting overly heated about them, where you could disagree and still remain friends.

Usually.

I was in touch with my younger brother, Ben. He came up from Philadelphia regularly to meet with the Sons of Liberty in Boston and Dunster. I met with him at the tavern, once he explained why Elizabeth had left John. When I understood, I could forgive her the pain she caused. In fact, it seemed that John deserved it . . .

But back to Samuel Adams. What did the fellow really want? He had convinced Ben and men like him that protecting our charter rights was the only thing he was trying to do.

See here, I understand that these tax acts do seem to undermine our rights, but it's only temporary! Until His

Majesty's indebtedness from the war is brought under control, I believe we must all pitch in and help. Once that's taken care of, everything will go back to normal—

But I think Samuel Adams doesn't want everything to go back. I think Sam Adams is moving us in the direction of declaring independence from England.

He is a traitor.

And his followers? Is Adams just using them?

Ben has brought Elizabeth with him to Dunster and after John's funeral, his friend, Tyler Moore, has come to the house, along with his helper Anton what's-his-name, asking me to go along with their cockamamie plan to bring back Lady Lisabet. (This, you understand, means Elizabeth). They want to establish her in John's Boston house and get her back into Boston society. As Lady Lisabet, she might invite her Tory friends here, to see if she can catch wind of a plot.

She could learn about what was going on by listening in a hidden closet I'd known nothing about. She would report back to Moore, and the Sons of Liberty would dismantle the plan somehow. With gunpowder plots, maybe, or assassinations, or disclosures that would arouse the colonials—all colonials—to rise up take over the government themselves.

Isn't that what Sam Adams really wants? To take over government?

That is treason.

Betsy and I talked it over. They want her to go to John's Brattles Street house with them, her and Sally, to provide the man-power (or, should I say, woman-power) to make the scheme work (an aristocratic lady always has servants, you see.)

Betsy is happy to go. And Sally is thrilled, because Anton what's-his-name will be in the house too. Both of my women did me the courtesy of waiting upon my decision, as though they would stay home if I said 'no'.

But I have played along, giving my permission, telling them I'll hire in help for the children and get the house ready in case Lady Lisabet invites her friends here—as long as Betsy promises to visit every fortnight. With that promise I can keep track of what Ben and his friends are up to. Betsy will tell me everything as we sit by the hearth of an evening chatting, me drinking rum, her drinking wine, sharing all the Boston doings with me. The more wine, the more details.

For if they are traitors, Ben's friends, and even if Ben himself is one, I'll have to report them, and stop them in their tracks. As a loyal subject of His Majesty, I can do no less.

God save the King!

Elizabeth Returns

Boston

A week after we had secured Tom's agreement to let Betsy and Sally help, and to use the Dunster house as bait, we were ready to begin. Sally and Anton and I, dressed in as citified a manner as we could contrive at such short notice, took the stage to Boston, leaving Annie and Paul behind with Sally's mother and her many boys.

It was a pleasant day, the beginning of summer with its fiercely blue skies, the gulls drifting high above, content in the sun. My old friend, Gwen Carter, stood in the doorway of her pretty two storied house, too impatient to wait within for her man-servant to announce the arrival of Lady Hopewell.

"Oh, Lizabet, my darling!" she squealed, her arms open wide. She drew me into the entry while Anton and Sally demurely waited on the steps.

"Gwen, dearest!" I exclaimed in Lady Lisabet's twittering voice. "How well you look!"

I held her at arms length, the better to view the entirety of her. She had certainly not wasted away while I was gone! As Lady Lisabet, I said, "I trust you received my letter, telling you I wished to visit."

"I did, indeed! I was so thrilled to learn you had come back to us!"

I turned to Anton. "May I present my cousin, Antoine duBois Hopewell de Montaigne?"

"Madame." Anton stepped up and into the entry and bowed over Gwen's extended hand. "Enchanté."

"Ooooh! Moi aussi!" Gwen was thrilled to meet a member of the French aristocracy, and indeed, Anton dressed up nicely as a highborn duke or marchioness or whatever he was supposed to be. (I couldn't quite remember. It was a detail we had rehearsed on the way from Dunster, but I was too absorbed in recalling Lady Lisabet's mannerisms to pay much attention. We would work on it later, until I could say it automatically, should anyone ask. And they would. The Trinity Crowd loved the idea of aristocracy.)

"And this is my personal maid, Mistress Palmer." I brought Sally forward. Carter's servant closed the door.

"Why, I remember her!" Gwen exclaimed. "From before you left. We were at your country place and she helped with the table and brought us tea in the garden. How pleasant to see you again, my dear!"

Sally curtseyed. "Thank you, Ma'am."

"Please, let's go into the receiving room. You come too, Miss Sally. Smyth, please see to it that tea brought immediately."

The servant nodded and disappeared.

"I see you persuaded your darling Donald to get you a chandelier." I pointed to the one in the entry. "Donald is

Madam Carter's husband," I told Anton, then turned back to Gwen. "I remember your being impressed with the one in Madeleine's house. Very pretty!"

"What a good memory you have, Milady!" Gwen cooed, seating everyone by gesture as she spoke. "There, I think we can all be comfortable now."

"I can, if you stop being so formal," I reproved. "'Milady', indeed. It's not as though we don't already know one another, my dear Gwen."

"No, of course not!"

"And Donald? How is he?"

"Better than ever."

"And Madeleine, and her husband. Was his name Thomas? Such lovely people."

"Lovely no longer," Gwen Carter retorted. "They are both homespun Whigs now. No longer one of us."

"Good gracious!" I exclaimed. "Whigs! How astonishing! Philadelphia is Tory territory, so Antoine and I have had little contact with individuals of inappropriate political persuasion. I wouldn't know what to say to a Whig. Or about one."

"*C'est vrai.* It is true," Anton nodded. "We have had no practice. Your tutoring, Madame Carter, will be necessary in order to avoid *faux pas.*"

"What is a fo paw?" Sally asked, forgetting her role as a servant.

"A social blunder," I told her, and she giggled, covering her mouth prettily though she still had all her teeth.

"I can't imagine Mr. Antoine blundering anywhere, any time," she tittered.

We all laughed in the merry fashion of the privileged. "I am still training her," I explained to Gwen as the tea arrived, giving Sally and Anton and me a respite from this, our first foray into spying.

"I do want to explain, dear Gwen," I went on, "about just—disappearing—so long ago."

"Certainly you are not obliged to explain yourself to me, my dear. You've returned. Nothing else matters."

"So kind. But soon enough I will need your help—and there is no reason for you to render it when I have been so thoughtless."

"I will help you, explanation or not," Gwen Carter promised loyally, adding, "though I would like to know what happened, naturally."

Lady Lisabet was on her feet so fast no one even thought to rise with her. "It was my little Paul," I said in my best Lady Lisabet voice, pacing, wringing my hands. "He was very frightened at the noise of the soldiers marching and the drums beating and the commanders shouting, on and on. Do you remember that—when they first came to Boston?"

"Indeed I do."

"He became so upset that he got sick. Couldn't breathe properly—oh, goodness, Gwen, it was so frightening. The doctor thought it was caused by a constriction of the throat that prevented sufficient air from getting to his lungs."

"Oh, my dear. How awful. But you never said he was unwell."

"It happened quickly. One day he was fine, the next he was turning blue."

"Terrible. More tea?"

"Thank you." I seated myself again. "The doctor thought his fear tightened everything up, you see. Then appeared Antoine's father, my uncle, passing through from Quebec City. When he saw Paul's condition, he fairly scooped us up, Paul and me, and off we went to Philadelphia."

"Indeed," remarked Gwen. "And Philadelphia agreed with him?"

"He loved it. In fact I left him there when I went back to Europe, to see my family and friends. Our relatives adored him and he had all manner of cousins to play with."

"How nice," she cooed.

"When I returned to America, the social demands were great. The Quakers hardly interfere with the Upper Orders, so it's as gay as London there."

"*Vraiment!*" Anton added. "The Quakers, they dance not. And come not to entertainments musical and theatric."

"We hated to leave, but I had to attend to John's estate."

"Now I am terribly embarrassed." Gwen blushed. "I have entirely overlooked sharing my condolences with you. John's death was very quick, was it not?"

"So quick that Antoine and Paul and I barely made it up to Dunster in time for the burial. As you see, we had time to bring only a few articles of clothing! La! Such a disgrace!" I made deprecating gestures toward our dishabille.

"You could wear a rag, Lisabet, and no one would notice. How can I help, my dear?"

"Well, when I was gone, John went back to Dunster to live for a while. He rented our house here in Boston to some British officers. We gave them notice and they have gone, but the place needs refurbishing—I can't possibly entertain with it looking as it does—but I must be nearby to oversee the details. Sally needs to get my clothes out of storage and start altering them, and she needs a place to sew. Antoine will fend for himself, sleeping wherever he can while the work is in progress, but Sally and I—well— do you suppose we might stay with you until John's house is ready?"

The three of us waited, hardly daring to breathe, to see if Gwen would accommodate us by slipping into the snare we had set.

"Oh, gracious, I would be honored!" She clapped her hands gleefully, and the three of us exhaled in unison.

We played on that stage long enough to get Lady Lisabet re-established and her wardrobe refurbished. Antoine Hopewell de Montaigne was introduced to society and tentatively accepted (after all he was French! A little caution was called for!) and Gwen took Lady Lisabet here and there and old friends invited them to tea.

At the end of the three week hiatus, the house on Brattles Street was painted inside and out, its furnishings cleaned, beaten or laundered, draperies hung, carpets laid. Paul's nursery changed into to a big-boy's bedroom. An alcove in the master chamber was outfitted for Annie.

Betsy brought the children to me, riding in John's coach, pulled by John's horses, driven by Sam who was now free, and who agreed to act as groom and coachman to Lady

Lisabet. If we needed to go back to Dunster at a moment's notice, he'd be on hand to take us there. And Betsy had promised to visit Tom every fortnight. Sam would get her to Dunster and back whenever she asked to go.

Now that I had suitably elegant clothing and a carriage and a man-servant to drive it, I could start to live the life of an unattached, well-bred upper-crust woman who drank endless cups of tea with her friends, was escorted to dinner parties and dances by her handsome cousin, and best of all, taken to the best commercial establishments in Boston for that most enduring of female amusements: shopping.

When I was married to Squire John, he selected the fabric, colors and trims I would wear as Lady Lisabet. He assumed I wouldn't know how the Better Sort dressed, and although I had observed the upper classes when I lived in England, I didn't know enough. John was right.

He had hired a seamstress to come to the house, bringing fabric samples and sketches and fashion dolls until I had as complete a wardrobe as I'd need. Just then we were content to wait, Paul grew bigger and we could add a few months to his age. It was time well spent, creating Lady Lizabet Hopewell and making Paul appear legitimate.

And now Milady wished to go shopping, buying her own fabrics and choosing her own styles. On this particular day I picked up Caroline Cunningham. Over tea the week before, she'd offered to take me to Roberge Imports.

"I've already selected some nice linens," she said as Sam wheeled us down Hanover Street toward the market.

(Having Sam at the reins always impressed my upper class friends. And Sam was, in fact, quite imposing in his livery.) "For our dining room," Caroline went on. "I hope the monograms I commissioned are finished!"

"I hope so, too," I agreed with the sort of semi-smile aristocrats favored. "I should enjoy seeing them."

"My husband, Ronald, says I may order drapery materials now. He has sketches of our new house, so I can judge pretty accurately how much we'll need."

"Oh?" I queried politely, as might be expected. "Your new house?"

"Yes, indeed. We are building it in Roxbury. The foundations are already being dug, and soon the construction will commence."

"Won't you miss the others?"

"What others?"

"Your friends here."

"Oh! Many of them are building outside the city, too, in one hamlet or another, close by Boston so the men will need only take a horse to town. It will be splendid, Milady. We'll have formal gardens and heated chambers—like yours in Dunster!"

"Our estate is simply a renovated farmhouse, dear Caroline. You will outdo me! La!"

"No one will ever outdo you, Lady Lisabet!"

"Clearly, you are going to try!" I watched closely as I asked, "And will you be able to move into the new house soon?"

"As soon as . . . " She stopped, glanced covertly at me. "Oh, look!" She pointed toward the harbor, where warships rode at anchor. "I find them so impressive! I'm thrilled every time I see them! They are a reminder of His Majesty's power, are they not?"

"Indeed," I agreed in what I believed would be Lady Lisabet's approbation.

"Sometimes I envy your being born there," Caroline sighed. "In England."

"None of us has much to say about where we were born, dear girl!" I laughed lightly as Lady Lisabet would, and thought: she stopped. Right in the middle of telling me when she and her husband would move into their mansion. What are they waiting for?

"Look, we're here!" Caroline announced.

And yes, we were pulling up to the door of Roberge Imports. Sam jumped down, opened the carriage door and unfolded the step, helped us down. "Shall I wait, Ma'am?" he asked.

Of course the carriage hopelessly blocked the narrow street, but if he took it down to the wharf area, which was quite broad in order to accommodate business, he would not know when to return.

The shopkeeper appeared at the door. "Is there a problem? Oh, good day, Mistress Cunningham!"

"Mistress Roberge." They exchanged courtesy dips. "We are trying to think of how the driver will know when to return, if he takes my friend's carriage down to the wharf."

Sam tipped his coachman's hat.

"Perhaps he could walk back in—say—an hour's time and see how we progress."

"Very well. You may walk back in an hour," I said imperially to Sam.

"Yes'm."

Returning the steps to their rightful place, he climbed up onto his elevated seat and set off. He was enjoying himself, I knew. And I liked having him nearby, in case of need.

Caroline introduced the shop owner, Mistress Margaret Roberge. Bows and curtsies and how-do-you-does were exchanged. Within, shelves lined the walls, with clearly labeled boxes on them. The closed containers kept the fabrics from getting dusty, Mistress Roberge explained.

In a sunny spot, wines, richly glowing, were displayed. They were French, she told us, and the laces were French, too. The linens were Irish, produced by her distant Huguenot relatives.

"I was telling Lady Lisabet that the monograms on my new table linens might be ready," Caroline suggested.

Mistress Roberge signaled her clerk, and while the monogrammed linens were being fetched, led us to a small sitting area where we could take our ease while looking at samples of lace. The finished monograms were were shown—and they were superlative.

"Who do you get to do such magnificent work?" I querried.

"It's a trade secret, Milady," Mistress Roberge smiled, and then asked, "Shall I address you as Lady Hopewell, Ma'am? Or Lady Rawlings?"

"These things are so complicated, are they not?" I drawled. "I can't be Lady Rawlings, because my husband was not a knight. I haven't been a Hopewell since marrying him, yet I am usually identified in that manner."

"It doesn't matter what anyone calls her," Caroline said, in a tone meant to comfort. "We're just glad to have her back."

"Caroline and I, and several other ladies of the Trinity Set, have known one another for quite a while," I told the proprietress. "Truly delightful. And this is such a delightful establishment. You are naughty, Caroline, not to have brought me here before."

"La!" Caroline exclaimed meaninglessly. "We were busy welcoming His Majesty's officers, if you'll remember!"

I shuddered as visibly as possible. "It was amusing at first, when they came to town. But then—the noise!" I explained Paul's presumed aversion to Mistress Roberge.

"Now we have her back, just in time to give us advice about our new houses," Caroline explained.

"Oh?" queried Mistress Roberge. "Lady Hopewell has a new house also?"

"She has a wonderful place in the country that has been in her husband's family for many years. We loved it."

"Perhaps all of you should come for a visit again, my dear," I said. It was not the best time to bring up the subject, but Caroline had led right into it, and I dared not let the opportunity pass.

"Oh! What a wonderful idea," she cried. "It would refresh our recollections as we start decorate and landscape our own places. Your gardens were just so lovely.

And several of our newer friends have never even been there. Perhaps we might bring one or two of them along?"

"If they are friends of you and Ronald, they'll be most appropriate. And I suppose Gwen and . . ."

"I'm not sure about the Carters . . ."

"Really!"

"Well, these days you have to think ahead, into the future. Neither Gwen nor Donald seem able to do that."

"Indeed."

"We'd most likely invite the Worthingtons, whom you don't know, but will enjoy, I am sure. And the Hempsteads. You may remember them."

Mistress Roberge had looked on as this discussion went forward, but was getting restless now. "My clerk and I can assemble samples for your draperies while you make your plans," she suggested sweetly.

"Lovely. Please bring them over here." The bemused look on Caroline's face told me she was probably still thinking about the guest list.

Boxes began to pile up as I said, "Dear, you must remind the men that our dining room is very advantageous for card games and such. We ladies can amuse ourselves while they play. It might make visiting more attractive to them.

"No doubt," said Caroline, digging into the nearest box. "Perhaps we ladies would even prefer to be left alone for a while!"

She was happy. As was I.

The bait had been taken.

The rest of the morning passed while I watched her going through samples of materials and trims.

How soon could we get the house in Dunster ready?

Could the gardens be made to look fine again?

CHAPTER NINE

The Party

In fact, Tom had been busy around the place ever since we left. Ben had stayed to help, and between them and assistance from the local Sons of Liberty, the garden was properly weeded, the bushes clipped, statuettes washed and carefully repositioned, paving slates aligned. The four chimneys were whitewashed and a bold black ring had been painted around the top of each, announcing Tory sympathies within. The fireplaces were cleaned and wood baskets were filled with tinder and smallish logs that would catch quickly but not burn too long.

Wives of the Sons aired sheets and blankets, made up the beds, washed and waxed the floors, readied the commodes. In the dining room the cabinets twinkled with clean crystal goblets and cut glass pitchers; table linens were washed and pressed, every piece of china we possessed shining, all flatware gleaming.

Caroline and her husband had known almost immediately who they wanted to invite. Arrangements were made for departure, and within the week a flotilla was formed: Anton and me in my carriage driven by Sam (being of the nobility, I did not share my ride!) Next came Margaret Hempstead and her husband Reginald with the new couple, Ebinizer Worthington and his wife Eleanor, followed by Caroline Cunningham and her husband, Ronald, and Marietta Johnston and her spouse Walter. Cunningham had volunteered his own wagon for the trunks, not just of the party goers but of their servants, who followed our parade in the Johnston family conveyance. The servants, of course, included Sally, with whom I had spent a good deal of time planning the details of the outing.

"Even if you don't find anything amiss, or a plot of some kind," she pointed out, "it puts you exactly where you want to be in their social circle. The gracious aristocrat, willing to share her lovely country home."

"Yes, yes, yes," I agreed. "But I don't know what to do with them! When all of us were there last, an elephant was on tour, and there was a Guy Fawkes bonfire on the village common—"

"I remember!" she laughed.

"Nothing is happening just now. No elephant. No parade. Will they want to just sit around? Do nothing?"

"They never do anything anyway, Aunt Elizabeth, but I think I can provide entertainment for at least one afternoon. My friend Mary Dodge loves to read palms. Pretend fortunes, you know. She can't do it very often because the minister might find out—"

We both knew what a commotion this would raise, "pretend" or not.

"But your Boston folks don't know the minister and aren't likely to say anything to anyone anyway—we could make a stage play of it." Since learning about Boston's attitude toward the theater, Sally was reveling in what she considered to be her daily performance as a spy. "Mary can put on her gypsy costume and bring her tambourine and dance, and read everyone's palm when she's done."

"Dance?"

"Like a real gypsy. We can have chairs set up outside, just beyond the keeping room so that the ladies can be seated if they wish, or not, and the maids can gather 'round too. That way, if a few of us come and go, it will hardly be noticed."

"Like me? Stealing into the closet?"

"Exactly like that."

"And if it rains?"

"We'll just have to use the keeping room itself, and keep our voices down."

Not much chance of that, I thought. "The men will certainly want us to leave them, don't you think?"

"Of course. And once they're settled in the dining room, they'll be committed and can't very well come back out. Even when something interesting is happening."

"And once Mistress Dodge comes, I'll slip into the closet. You can fetch me if there's any reason I should come out."

"What shall we do about Anton? The men won't want him at any meeting."

"Sam can take him for a ride in the carriage. He's new to the area, being from Philadelphia and all. Needs to see what's here."

Anton and Sam agreed.

There was going to be an unexpected visitor, Ebin Worthington told me just after breakfast. Arriving in the afternoon to join the gentlemen. Would that be agreeable?

"Unfortunately there is no plan for anyone extra," I told him with as much hauteur as I could summon. "We shall not be able to accommodate your friend for dinner or lodging. Out of the question."

"He'll arrive mid-afternoon, so will need nothing from your kitchen. And his man will drive him home when we are finished with our meeting."

"Very well," I agreed slowly, "If you're sure he can take care of himself."

"I am, Milady. He'll be no trouble at all."

After the main meal at noon, the ladies and I excused ourselves so that the men could smoke and drink claret, as men always did. The hired help (Tom) had already fetched extra chairs, setting them in a semi-circle in front of a low bench on which tea could be served. The gypsy's performance would take place just beyond, in a space easily visible to all.

We busied ourselves with tea and chatter, wandering about as we waited for Mistress Dodge. The serving girls hovered nearby with refreshments from the keeping room. There was a lot of ongoing activity as a result.

When the front door knocker resounded through the house, it fell to me, the hostess, to let the stranger in, since my serving girl was pouring tea in the garden and my coachman-valet was riding around the neighborhood with the Frenchman.

Standing there was a robust gentleman, clad in silks and sporting lace collar and cuffs. On the road in front of the house was a chaise, horse and driver.

Bowing, he removed his hat. "Lady Lisabet Hopewell, I presume?"

I curtseyed in reply.

"I am Richard Akwright, Madam. Your friends invited me to meet them here. I hope that doesn't inconvenience you."

"No, indeed! Tell your man there's a public trough for the horse at the Inn yonder."

He waved to the fellow, pointed, and the driver led the horse in the correct direction. No doubt this possibility had been discussed already.

The door to the dining room was immediately to my right. I opened it and waved him through, closed it quickly and waited, listening.

Congenial greetings were exchanged, Mr. Awkright seated, rum distributed. I stole into the closet, scarcely daring to breathe—but I needn't have worried. Five men make a lot of noise. Ebin Worthington had taken the head of the table and Mr. Akwright occupied the foot, his back to me.

They all turned to look out the window at the young woman who walked by just then, wearing a meager black dress and a scarlet drape over her shoulders and an immense scarlet sash wound around her head, approximating a turban. Great exclamations arose from the ladies and the

serving girls. Quickly all of them took their places. Mistress
Dodge must have been carrying Spanish clickers, for I could
hear them from the closet, and then she started to sing in a
throaty, strangulated voice—like a squawk—and presum-
ably began to dance.

Through the closet's crack I saw the men turning to
their own business, and I heaved a slow sigh of relief.

Seated on either side of the table, the husbands removed
their coats and hung them from their chair-backs; two of
them rolled up their sleeves. From my vantage point in the
closet, I could see that Worthington, at the far end, was
unhappy with this informality.

"Don't ever do that when you're in England," he warned.

"If we're ever in England," grumbled Reginald Hempstead.

"Well, that rather depends on what role you're willing to play in the new Order. If you're one of the Knights
Companion, you'll likely go at some point. It is from that
group that representatives to Parliament will be chosen."

"Who by?"

"The Oligarchy can vote on it, if that's how we decide.
Or we can decide that the Supreme Oligarch will select a
knight each year, but I'm a little reluctant to vest that much
power in any one person. I'm in favor of the whole Oligarchy
voting."

"Each year?"

"Each year."

"We're getting ahead of ourselves," complained Walter
Johnston.

"Indeed we are," said Awkright at the foot of the table. "I didn't come all this way to bicker over the details. It's an excellent meeting place, by the way. Do you suppose Lady Hopewell would allow us to use it on regular occasions? No one from Boston would know, if we met here. And we could stay at the Inn, so that Milady wouldn't be incommoded."

"If that's what we decide we want to do, I'd be glad to find out," Ronald Cunningham offered.

"Then let's get started." Worthington called the meeting to order. "The most pressing topic is your willingness to take the bottom-most rung on British aristocrat ladder in order to be top-most here."

"I don't like it," growled Awkright. "It's demeaning."

"Only if you're British. But we're not," argued Walter Johnston. "It's not at all demeaning if we decide it isn't."

"That's absolutely true," agreed Hempstead. "It's aristocracy, fellows. An American Aristocracy. There's nothing demeaning about that!"

"And we are free to do whatever we like," Worthington cajoled. "No one in England will care, as long as we pose no threat to them."

"Threat indeed!" one of them chuckled, and they all laughed.

Mistress Dodge, forsaking her clickers, flashed past the window waving her red shawl as though a bull had just entered the garden. Her turban was starting to unwind and its tails trailed behind her as she circled the birdbath, fending off the bull.

"Are we in agreement, then? That we accept our position as the lowest component in the English pecking order?"

Unanimous ayes were heard.

"Richard? Are you sure about it?" Worthington asked. "You've got to be sure."

"Yes, yes," Awkright confirmed bruskly.

"Very good. The next item on the list is who we choose to be elevated to the position of Supreme Oligarch. And we'll need to choose a designated successor to the title."

"Why?"

"It takes the place of primogeniture. The Supreme Oligarch is a baronet, which isn't a hereditary title, but succession must be assured since the Order holds letters patent. We can comply by designating a successor at the same time that the Supreme Oligarch is chosen."

"I volunteer," said Awkright, "for the position of Supreme Oligarch. Not that Ebin wouldn't be fine. After all, he's done all the work so far. But I know Bellingham— the Earl of Stanwick— personally, and have met a few other important men through him, and I suspect I understand the English way of doing things better than Ebin does."

The group appeared nonplussed at Awkright's temerity, and passed the rum jug to distract themselves. The performance outside had stopped and was replaced by the babble of women as they arranged themselves for the fortune-telling.

Ebin cleared his throat. "Well, as long as we are nominating ourselves, I declare my candidacy here and now. I have brought the plan to completion and have the necessary contacts in England and here in the colonies. I think there can be no question about who should be supreme."

"I second that," said Walter Johnston, sneaking a peek out the window.

"We'll have to pass the hat," Ebin said. "I've brought a pencil, and a few pieces of paper." These he held up—small squares.

"Here," offered Awkright, reaching for his hat which he had laid on the floor beside his chair.

The paper squares were passed out. The pencil, and then the hat, followed. There was a long pause while the voting proceeded, then ended with Ebinezer Worthington who scribbled on his square and dropped it into the hat. Shaking it, he placed it in front of him on the table and took each square out, one by one. Read the name on it, put it in a pile, one for him, one for Awkright.

His pile grew. Awkright's didn't.

"Six votes myself. Two for Richard. I think it's conclusive, gentlemen, and I thank you for your confidence. I'll write it up and get it notorized and give it to the Earl. And I'd like to propose that Richard be selected the successor to the baronetcy. All in favor, signify by saying "Aye".

Everyone said it.

Whether Awkright was mollified by this, I'm sure no one could tell. Perhaps no one cared.

"I'll include that information, too. Well, then!" Worthington's face shone. "Here are some papers you must sign as Knights Companion. We're allowed ten total, and so, as you see, there are five more that we'll fill in when we decide who else shall be on the council."

"And fifteen Least Oligarchs, is that correct?" Cunningham asked.

"Just so. Be thinking about the men who can best connect with the Loyalists here in Massachusetts Bay. And you all had better finish up building your country estates, so you'll be ready to entertain gentlemen and ladies from the other colonies."

"Have you figured out yet how let our wives know they won't be up to snuff, when it comes to entertaining the English Upper Crust?" asked Walter Johnston.

"Perhaps we needn't invite anyone from England, at least not right away." Hempstead suggested.

"Indeed. We can just entertain each other and the new knights until we see how the land lies," Ronald Cunningham said. "It will take a while to re-organize the government, after all."

"That's a good point," Ebin assured him. "Then, when we're ready, we can start with the upper crust right here in America, who needn't know how low we are. They'll only see how elevated we've become!"

"Hear! Hear!" they called, and drank.

In the closet, I held myself up by a coat peg and breathed deeply, to calm myself. Their elevation was arranged already and in one way or another, they were going to take over.

"How are those damn Committees of Correspondence working out?" Worthington asked. "The ones Sam Adams insisted we needed?"

"They're spreading all over the colonies."

"Maybe the Least Ollie Garks can get appointed soon so they can work with the Loyalists and put an end to it," Hempstead declared. "At least here in Massachusetts."

I didn't wait for the subsequent discussion. Leaving the closet, I crept quietly down the hall, through the keeping room and out to the ladies and girls now huddled around Mistress Dodge, whose turban lay in a scarlet heap while she read their palms. I don't think they even noticed when I rejoined them.

I'd have to send Sam back tonight, or at dawn. I didn't know what the Sons of Liberty could do about the growing danger of what sounded like a takeover, but the sooner they knew about it, the better. Sam Adams was inalterably opposed to murder, but perhaps Worthington's departure with his official papers could be delayed by one means or another, perhaps indefinitely. Broken windows at his business. Sabotage by his domestic staff at home, all of whom were patriots. Intercepted mail. And, when all was said and done, perhaps fate would intervene, and the new Order would never come to pass.

We would do our best and hope the Almighty would intervene in our favor.

Winter 1773

CHAPTER TEN

The Supreme Oligarch

Stanwickshire, England

E binezer Worthington was clearly disturbed.
     "My Lord," he exclaimed upon entering the presence of the Earl, forgetting to bow or wait for a greeting from his host. "The situation in Boston is unravelling fast. I only hope that we can get the Order established before there's an outright rebellion."

The Earl turned to his hovering servant. "Rum," he ordered. "The whole jug, if you please. Be seated, Worthington, and contain yourself," he said to Ebin. He tried to envision a meeting of American Aristocrats facing a crisis. It appeared certain that one was coming their way. An unwanted image of hens fluttering noisily about their enclosure came to mind.

"What is the issue now?" he asked wearily.

"Last fall Samuel Adams and a friend set up a committee of Correspondence at the Boston Town Meeting. Do you know what those are?"

"I do. Such committees have been used before, I believe, to clarify confusion over one law or another. They disband once the problem is resolved."

"Very good. No need to explain them to you. Now, you must be familiar with the recent decision to have the salaries of the royal governor and judges be paid by the Crown rather than the colonial assemblies."

"Yes. A holdover from the Townshend Acts, I believe."

"And because it has now been dug up and reactivated, the colonies have no means of holding public officials accountable to their constituents."

"True."

"The Boston Committee of Correspondence was introduced by Samual Adams in response to this. He's got a lot of committees in the towns and villages of Massachusetts, too."

"Why was I not informed before now?" demanded the Earl. "This could be serious."

"This *is* serious. I wrote you, sir. You, however, never answered."

"I received no letter. You should have come, yourself."

"This is the earliest I could. So much has been happening! Windows broken in my storehouse. My place of business set on fire. Our house servants malingering. Disgusting things left on our doorstep. I couldn't leave Boston without making suitable arrangements for my wife."

"I understand," Bellingham consoled. "And all these Committees of Correspondence are instigated by Samuel Adams, I take it? Can no one stop this man? Arrest him? Send him over here for trial?"

"He is close to treason, but does not cross the line," Ebin explained, head in his hands.

Bellingham's servant arrived with the rum. "Bring over a small table and set it here," the Earl instructed. "And bring my whiskey decanter, please."

A little early, perhaps, but the occasion seemed to warrant it.

"And the other colonies are beginning to do the same," Ebinizer moaned. "So that all of them will know what the others are thinking. And now, the Tea Act. You can hear the pens scratching from here! Is the Act entirely necessary, My Lord? This is a bad time to prove Parliament can tax us if it chooses. And shipping East India tea to the Colonies, to be sold at a lower price than smuggled tea? A little incendiary, I'm afraid, sir."

"It's more than proving Parliament's power, dear fellow. The American boycott of English tea has nearly bankrupted the East India Company. It is on the verge of collapse. We cannot allow that to happen; we need its income badly. So, yes, I'd say both the act and the reduced rate tea was necessary. We can raise the price once the colonists get so accustomed to it that they'll refuse anything else."

"I wouldn't count on it. Now that they have these damned committees, they can explore the alternatives together. They may even decide to resist as has been the case before—but now better organized. We must put the American Oligarchy in place now, and declare the Massachusetts Committees illegal. Arrest their members, if necessary. Use them as an example."

"Oh, Christ," blasphemed the Earl as he thought about the ramifications. "Did you bring the papers with the necessary signatures?" he asked, massaging his temples.

"Yes, I have them with me. Including my election as leader. And the rest of the money we pledged, too."

"Very well. In a private ceremony, His Majesty will proclaim you Supreme Oligarch whenever we request it. If he can give us three minutes today, then we'll do it today. We got you a copy of the letters patent that give legitimacy to the Order, and we'll see that there's a royal order that requires General Gage to assist you in breaking up this situation."

"General Thomas Gage?" The commander of all military forces in the American colonies.

"If you want to arrest everyone who belongs to a Committee of Correspondence all over your colony, you'll need an army to do it."

Ebin gulped. "Yes. I suppose I will."

"I'll have my attics searched for an appropriate garment to wear at your presentation to His Majesty. We've already packed the medallions and sashes you asked for, and the copy of the letters patent and the gubernatorial appointment. There are ships loading now with tea from the East India Company, and if your elevation can be arranged today, you can sail back on any one of them and be in Boston almost before anyone knows you left."

"That may well be true. We are careful, My Lord, to keep our comings and goings obscured."

"Perfect. My men will take everything to the docks while we are with His Majesty, and then I'll see you on your way. No time I waste! The sooner you and your associates are in place, the sooner you can counteract these Committees of Correspondence."

"Indeed!" Ebin puffed up with importance and pleasure.

"Who will be your designated successor, by the way?"

"Awkright. And he'll represent us in Parliament, too."

"He'll do well there. I look forward to seeing him again."

Ebin sat back, refilled his rum. "So it'll really happen," he sighed. "I'm going to be an aristocrat!"

Such a pet he was, observed Bellingham, so pleased with the prospect of his new title that temporarily, at least, he seemed able to overlook the fact that bringing Gage into the mix could start a war.

Perhaps he didn't care.

CHAPTER ELEVEN

Sam

Aslave, he part of the furniture. He see everything, he hear everything, he know everything, becuz folks forget he there.

I always be slave, becuz my mama was. After Masta John die, his brudda, Tom, he own me along with cow and horse and carriage. But Masta Tom, he don't want me. Not for bein owned. He say, "Sam, you're a free man now. I already signed paper that says so."

I beg him, burn up paper. I say, "Where can I go? Who my people? Black folks, they live one place, they live another place, they live in Boston. No black folks here in Dunstah. Please, sir, don't sign no paper."

"Suppose I sign it, but you stay here with us. Like we're your family," Masta Tom say. "I can hardly recall a time you haven't been with us, Sam."

Oh, it true.

Masta Tom, he hold out his hand.

I cry.

<hr/>

I been with them for as long as Masta John was crippled, and I watch after all of 'em even if they dint know it.

And when Masta John marry Miz Elizbet, I watch after her real careful, too, becuz she new here in 'Merica. Look so lost, so scared, gettin off that boat, goin to meet Masta. I feel her shakin when I hand her up into his carriage.

An I hep her run away, after Masta John beat her bad. An when Masta John hide her little boy, I hep her find him and take him away to . . . wherever it was she and Masta Ben go.

Later, when I am free man, she axed me would I pretend to be her servant when she took on being Lady Lisabet again. Mr. Tyler Moore axed me too. So I got to be Son of Liberty. Me! To hep Mr. Tyler Moore and Masta Ben take care of Miz Elizbet while she pretendin.

She go to Boston wid Miss Sally and Mr. Anton, and soon enuff I bring little Paul an baby Annie an Miz Betsy over from Dunstah. We all of us watch after the chilren while Miz Elizbet went out with the rich folks. I drive her to this house, that house, this shop, that one.

Then she have party for rich folk at the big house in Dunstah. I drive Mr. Anton aroun while Boston men meet in dinin room and Miz Elizbet listen to 'em. She write letter, send me to Mr. Tyler Moore. Then party over. We all come back to town. I go on drivin Mis Elizbet around until one day, when winter was startin, her frien Miz Cunningham come acallin, all by herself.

Me, I wuz gallumping around in the garden wid little Paul on my back. Miz Elizbet open receivin room winda, call in soft voice Sam! Sam! Come ansa door! Cuz she cant ansa her own self. High ladies don't ansa they own doors.

Miz Betsy come take Paul upstairs. I pull down my coat an smooth it best I can, pull up my stockins, go quick to front door while Miz Elizbet fetch tea pot an cups.

"I must see Lady Lisabet!" Miz Cunningham cried, tears arunnin down her face. "Please ask if she will receive me!"

"Yes'm." She wait while I go into receivin room where Miz Elizbet hurryin to arrange her hair an fishu an skirts, tryin to look like she got all the time in the world.

"She very upset, Miz Cunninham is," I tell her. "She not notice if you in nightgown."

"The show must go on," Miz Elizbet sigh. "Bring her in."

She rise up grand as Miz Cunninham come, bawlin and wiping eyes wit hankie. They hug. "You seem quite distraught, my dear," say Noble Lady. "Sit here, and let me pour you a cup of His Majesty's finest. This may be all we can get for a while."

Miz Cunninham sit but then jump back up, look out windows, look at me standin dumb as a stump behind Miz Elizbet's chair, sit again.

"Of all the people I know," she whisper, face all twisted, "you're the one I trust most."

"Speak up, Caroline!" order Miz Elizbet. "I can't hear you."

"You're the only one who can really understand. No patent. No medals. No sashes. No dubbing."

She start to cry again, an Miz Elizbet say, "Control yourself, Caroline! Control yourself. I insist. Breathe deeply. There! Just like that. Breathe. Breathe."

She do it, get quiet, put back shoulders, pick up tea cup.
It rattle on saucer. "Did you know there are three ships in
the harbor right now, filled with East India tea?"

"Yes, I did know. And there is a lot of squabbling about
whether the tea will be allowed to unload, or even allowed
to return to England, am I correct?"

"Yes. What you may not know is that there were four
ships bringing the tea. The *William* has gone down." She
breathe deep again. "On board were all the credentials for
an American nobility."

Miz Elizbet fill her cup again. "Please explain."

"Ebinezer Worthington—you must remember him
from your party—has been working out the details of a new
American aristocracy with His Majesty."

"An American aristocracy!"

"And Ebin went to England to get dubbed by the king.
He wrote us a letter that came on one of the other ships. He
said he had all the papers and seals and sashes . . ."

Her eyes fill up again, and we wait. She take deep, deep
deep breath. "He was on the ship that went down. The
William. Off the back of Cape Cod . . . do you know where
Cape Cod is, Milady?"

"I do."

"There were storms, and it got separated from the
others. They didn't know where it went. A man from Truro
sailed over and told everyone."

"That's too bad, I am sure," Milady said.

"The papers would have given us a man in Parliament.
Ebin Worthington would have been Royal Governor.

Ronald and our other friends were to form his council and
be Knights and get rich."

"Good grief, Caroline," Lady Lisabet exclaimed. "What
do you mean?"

"The taxes would be high enough to pay the colony's
share of the war debt, and the cost of running government
here. Once the war debt was paid, the tax would continue as
before. but His Majesty's portion would go to us. We would
have been so rich!"

Her eyes shine. Then fill wid water.

"But everything sank with that ship. Oh, Lady Lisabet,
now I have all those linens and drapes and there won't be
a house to put them in. We're in debt and we'll have to sell
everything we own."

Caterwallin begin again.

Miz Elizbet comfort her, say she find out if Hopewell
family can help, an somehow we get Miz Caroline out the
door. Then we just stand there, starin at each other.

"I think you ought to find Tyler Moore," she say. "Tell
him that he need not worry. The plot has failed."

"What mean 'plot'?"

"The Tory businessmen were planning a take-over
of government. That's the plot. But now it won't happen,
because that ship went down."

"*Willem.*"

"That's right."

"Do I go to Mr. Moore now?"

"Yes, please."

"Yes'm."

"Sometimes," she say, "one has to be grateful for divine help, don't you think? Like storms that come at the right time?"

"Yes'm," I agree. "Sometime. And sometime people have to get hep on they own."

"We could have done. But now we don't have to. Not yet."

No Colony take tea. Boston dump theirs into harbor. Ship go to England wid message about tea bein thrown out; ship come back four month later with letter from King. He say, PAY FOR TEA. Ship go back with message sayin NO.

Round about then dead man's wife come to door, all in black. "Eleanor!" say Lady Lisabet. "I hope you know how sorry I am about Ebin."

Dead man's wife start bawlin. "Oh, Lady Lizabet, I am so ashamed. It seems my husband brought a woman to Charles Town," she blubber. "From England. She says she'll tell everyone that she was his mistress, if I don't give her money. And I don't have any."

Lots of caterwallin then.

Sons of Liberty send bad woman in Charles Towne away.

Widow Worthington leave Boston too, never come back. No squallin no more.

Four month after rebels say NO to King, harbor closed. King say it stay closed til tea paid for. More

warships come. More soldiers come. Committees corre-
spond and colonies meet. There be Con-tin-en-tal Congress. Lot of talk. Lot of writin.

Militias get lot of practice.

Muskets get cleaned.

Rifles get sighted.

We go back to Dunstah, Masta Ben and Miz Elizbet
and Little Annie and Paul and Miss Sally an her modah
(who am Miz Betsy) and Mr. Anton and me.

Miss Sally and Mr. Anton marry at Dunstah church,
live in big house with Masta Tom and Miz Betsy and hep
wid all dem boys.

Miz Elizbet, Little Annie and Paul and me move into
Mr. Ben's house. It have pasture an river run nearby. A cow,
too old to give milk, live in leanto. Mr. Ben build extra
room for me so I don't have to sleep with cow. He and Miz
Elizbet get married in Masta Tom's parlor; then Mr. Ben
go back to Boston Town and Mr. S. Adams and then to
Genral Washinton.

Chilrens all go to school. Older boys learn to shoot;
two of they go to Washinton near end of war. One never
come back. We put stone in cemetery wid his name on it,
near Masta John's and his Pa and Ma an another Ma no
one like. She have stone anyway. A little one. It say 'Relict'
on it. There be another Ma stone, off to one side. That one
be Masta Ben's modda, waitin for him to keep her company.

I look after Miz Elizbet and the chilren while Mr. Ben
gone. When he come home, a leg missin, face have deep
lines in it, eyes sad. I hep him all I can.

Miss Margaret go to Ireland at start of war, take all hers an Tyler Moore's chilrens along. When war over he go there, to Ireland, so he can be Daddy again. No one say if he and wife like each other or not. I think maybe yes, cuz he stay there after last chile leave home.

Miz Sally an Mr. Anton, they go back to Acadia, that everbody call Nova Scotia now. They say it where Anton belong, even if he can't recall livin there.

Masta Tom an Miz Betsy don't have no chilren between them. I don't know why not. They be fit an healthy folk. But maybe they don't got no Divine hep.

Years, they roll on by.

And then, I get old. Miz Elizbet, she look after me. She say I lie next to her and Masta Ben in cemetery plot, between them and his modda, when I ready for it. An one day, Paul lie there too, wid his woman. An little Annie, if she not marry. An Masta Tom, and Miz Betsy.

All of us together.

They my family.

THE END

Afterword

No addendum would be complete without an apology to those readers who admire and respect the British peerage as a social system. As an American, I do not; however, I did strive to be as accurate as possible when dealing with Earls and Barons and baronets and letters patent and elevations to knighthood, etc. I'm sure I've failed, but I did want anyone whom I've offended to know I tried.

There's also a problem when the facts have to be manipulated to accommodate "alternative history." There is one instance of these in *The Traitors*. I didn't want to burden the manuscript with too many details but they are fascinating, and tell us a lot about Sam Adams. I'll describe it in detail when I start my blog, which can be found at

Deborahhillbooks.com

where other books by Deborah Hill are reviewed and may be purchased through Amazon.